LOVE AND
BETRAYAL
A NOVEL

Also by Muriel Maddox

Captain from Corfu
Llantarnam
Myra's Daughters
Noela & That Man in Rio

Love and Betrayal

A Novel

LOVE AND BETRAYAL

A Novel

by
Muriel Maddox

SUNSTONE
PRESS

First Edition

Printed and bound in the United States of America

Library of Congress Cataloging in Publication Data:

Maddox, Muriel.
    Love and betrayal: a novel / by Muriel Maddox.—1st ed.
        p. cm
    ISBN 978-0-86534-249-1 (hardcover) ISBN 978-1-63293-125-2 (softcover)
    1. Title.
PS3563. A339455L68   1996
813' .54—dc20   96-16304
                                                  CIP

Published by   SUNSTONE PRESS
                          Post Office Box 2321
                          Santa Fe, NM 87504-2321 / USA
                          (505) 988-4418 / *orders only* (800) 243-5644
                          FAX (505) 988-1025

To the memory of
Elliott Arnold

Grateful acknowledgment is made for permission to reprint from the following:

by Tennessee Williams, from *THE GLASS MENAGERIE*.
Copyright © 1945 by Tennessee Williams and Edwin D. Williams.
Reprinted by permission of New Directions Publishing Corp.

SOMEDAY I'LL FIND YOU, words and music by Noel Coward
© 1930 Chappell & Co. Ltd. Copyright Renewed
All Rights Reserved
Used by Permission
WARNER BROS. PUBLICATIONS INC., Miami, FL. 33014

"We only love what makes us suffer. . . ."
—*Gustave Flaubert*

ONE

T he seventh of July began like any other day for Peter Spaulding, with no hint of the tragedy ahead.

Midland was sweltering in a savage heat wave. Clouds of swirling red dust swept across the West Texas prairie, covering the parched brown grass and asphalt sidewalks of the town like layers of rust.

"Drive carefully, honey," Ruth Ellen said. She stood in the doorway, her pink cotton maternity smock sticking to her bloated body. Her ankles were swollen and her light brown hair was damp with perspiration. Beads of sweat formed on her upper lip. "You know I worry about you."

"I'll be all right."

He pulled out of the driveway. Ever since the accident she'd been nagging him. He was driving home from the oil fields and on a dangerous curve he had to swerve suddenly to avoid a truck that was coming straight at him. The car went out of control and the next thing he remembered was waking up in a ditch with a concussion.

He felt guilty about the sharpness of his voice and the hurt expression on Ruth Ellen's face. She was always trying to please him, she was patient and understanding when he got depressed and moody, it was not her fault that she wasn't his type and that he was always comparing her to Valerie and wishing that. . . .

What the hell good is wishing? he thought, and again he felt trapped.

"Midland is one of the last frontiers . . . a man can make a fortune there if he's lucky," he'd been told.

He'd arrived right after the war, twenty-six years old and determined to make it on his own. That was nearly two years ago. He had not made a fortune and the golden dream had disillusioned him. And now he was caught, choked with the smell of oil and sandstorms in this place with its newly-built skyscrapers rising like a mirage on the desolate plain.

He would never be a Texan as long as he lived, though sometimes, at first glance, he was taken for one because he was tall and lean and when he was in the oil fields he dressed like the natives and wore rumpled trousers and a sports shirt, with pointed Western boots and a light-colored Western hat. But the minute he spoke his voice gave him away. Well, he was tired of the drawling way they talked and the climate and having to pick sand out of his teeth all the time. Hell, you couldn't even barbecue a steak in your back yard unless you wanted it garnished with a fine coating of sand.

Texas. You can have it, he thought. All of it.

Oh, there were some pretty parts of Texas. The River Oaks section of Houston with its Colonial mansions and flowering redbud trees. Green grass and trees. How long it had been since he had seen anything green, like his father's place on the Eastern Shore of Maryland. "Wynwood" it was called. His father had sold it during the war. "Impossible to get servants to keep up the place," his father had written him. The letter reached him when he was fighting in Italy. He had hoped that someday Wynwood would be his and now it was gone. He had not even been consulted. It was typical of his father.

Yes, there were many reasons that had brought him to Midland. When he was discharged from the Army he had no home to go to. But then had he ever really had a home? he wondered. A real home?

He thought of his mother, now living in Rio de Janeiro. Senhora Roberto Moreiro Carvalho. Her picture appeared often in *Town and Country* and she always made the list of the Ten Best-Dressed Women. How hard she had tried to catch Roberto Carvalho after she divorced his father, and she finally succeeded where so many women before her had failed. For they said in Washington that Carvalho would never marry anyone. He was the Brazilian Ambassador then, handsome, sought after, and his affairs were notorious.

He remembered how nice Uncle Roberto was to him before he married his mother and how everything changed afterward. The Brazilian Embassy was never a home to him, only a brief stopover between boarding schools and summer camps.

This was the first home he had ever had and Ruth Ellen was the first person who had ever really believed in him. She was with him all the way. That's what made him feel so awful.

If only I loved Ruth Ellen the way I did Valerie, he thought. Or if only Valerie had loved me the way Ruth Ellen does.

Valerie. . . .

"All women are only good for a one-night stand," his father used to say. But then he was bitter after the divorce. He had never remarried. Lathrop Spaulding, the aging playboy, habitué of El Morocco and "21", he saw his father's name in the columns with this model and that showgirl. What was he trying to prove?

Or are we all trying to prove something?

She pulled into the parking lot beside him and rolled down the car window. Her flaming red hair was tied back with a ribbon and she had on dark glasses.

"Hi ya, handsome."

"Billie . . . what are you doing here?"

"I wanted to catch you before you went in the office and I didn't want to call you at home." She lowered her voice. "Listen, I have to talk to you."

"What about?"

"It's not about us. I know that's over."

He waited.

"I can't talk here. Meet me at my place."

"I don't think that's a very good idea."

"Look, he's out of town."

He wasn't about to get involved with this dame again. It wasn't fair to Ruth Ellen.

"It wasn't an accident," Billie said.

"What wasn't?"

"The car. It wasn't an accident. Now do you follow me?"

"Do you have any proof?"

"Yes. My place at noon?"

"All right," he said.

He walked in the Stanolind Oil offices with an uneasy feeling. He'd been in tight spots before and he'd always been lucky, but something told him his luck was running out. He tried to appear nonchalant, but he found he was perspiring and not just from the heat.

Mr. Garrison's secretary came up to him with a worried expression. "The boss would like to see you," she said.

Chet Garrison was a man of sixty who had come to Texas from Indiana. No matter how early you got to the office, he was always there first. He was studying a map on the wall of the latest drillings.

"Did you want to see me, sir?" Peter asked.

Garrison turned. He had a craggy, weather-beaten face under thinning gray hair and large hands with heavy calluses from his boyhood days on a farm. "Yes, I did." He motioned to a chair in front of his desk. "Sit down."

Peter wondered what was coming next. Garrison lit his pipe and then walked around and put his hand on Peter's shoulder.

"Are you in some kind of trouble?" he asked.

"I hope not, sir."

"You can level with me, my boy."

"I'm not sure what you mean."

"Yesterday two federal agents came in here and asked a lot of questions about you. I don't know what they were trying to find out." He paused "You know, I never had a son. Only daughters. Always wanted a son. If there is some way I can help . . . ."

"I appreciate that, sir." Now he was starting to have chills. He wondered how much Garrison knew.

"How's Ruth Ellen?"

"Pretty good. The heat's been getting her a bit."

"A nice girl. One of the best secretaries we ever had around here. You take good care of her, make her get plenty of rest. How much longer before the baby's due?"

"Five weeks. The middle of August."

"Say hello to her for me. Tell her we miss her."

"I will, sir."

"You're sure there's nothing you want to tell me?"

Peter shook his head. He wanted to get out of here, away from Garrison's probing look. Garrison trusted him, thought of him as the son he had never had, and he had let him down. There was a suffocating stillness in the room that was almost unbearable, and then the telephone rang.

"That's all, Peter."

Peter started toward the door.

"Remember, we all make mistakes." Garrison picked up the phone and started to talk to the person on the other end.

We all make mistakes.

He walked out of Garrison's office and down the corridor to the drinking fountain.

TWO

*B*illie stood in the bathroom doorway, her long red hair in disarray, a towel draped loosely around her. There was a triumphant smile on her face.

She dropped the towel and walked toward Peter.

"I'd better go," he said, reaching for his clothes.

She pushed him back on the bed and threw herself on top of him. "What's your hurry?"

"I shouldn't have come here in the first place. It isn't fair. . . ." He started to say to Ruth Ellen and then stopped. He didn't want to discuss her with Billie and he felt guilty as hell. He had never felt any physical excitement with Ruth Ellen, only a kind of tenderness, but that didn't make up for what was missing.

"It isn't fair to your wife, you mean?" Billie's voice was tinged with sarcasm. "If she was any good in the kip you wouldn't be here."

"Well don't think what just happened meant anything." He knew he was being cruel and he intended to be. "We've both been around, Billie. You know the score."

"So what the hell is that supposed to mean?"

"Take it any way you want." He pushed her off him. "Now let me get dressed."

She sat on the bed watching him.

In the mirror he noticed several long scratches running down his back from Billie's fingernails and he knew she had left her mark on him deliberately. That bitch, he thought. He never should have gotten mixed up with her in the first place. She spelled nothing but trouble.

"You men make me sick with your excuses," Billie said. "At least you don't pretend you love your wife. You don't love anyone."

He zipped his trousers. Love. Maybe his old man was right. All women were only good for a one-night stand. No, he had known love once. But she hadn't loved him enough. At least not enough to come to Midland with him. He wondered where she was now. Probably married. Well, why should it bother him? He was married. If you could call what he had with Ruth Ellen a marriage.

"You should at least be glad I'm concerned about your safety," Billie said. "You could have gone on thinking it was an accident."

"Billie, if someone's out to get me. ..." He shrugged. "There's not much I can do about it, is there?"

"Aren't you afraid?"

"I had too many near misses during the war. If a bullet has my number on it ... well, that's it." He finished buttoning his shirt. "But thanks for warning me."

"You're a cool customer."

"Listen, Billie, we've had a lot of fun together, but this mustn't happen again. I'm sure you realize that as well as I do."

"If you say so." She pushed a lock of hair out of her eyes and lit a cigarette.

"And you'd better put on some clothes. Just in case the milkman or someone comes to the door."

"Peter?"

"Yes?"

"Nothing. It's not important."

"Goodbye, Billie."

"See ya around, handsome."

❖

The car was like an oven and he quickly turned on the air conditioning and started the motor. A thick dust had settled on everything. He sometimes wondered why he ever bothered to wash his car. It was dirty again in a few hours. A matter of pride, he guessed.

There were times when he would like to strangle the Princeton classmate who first told him about Midland, but he wasn't around. He'd made his pile and moved back East.

I'll do that too, Peter thought.

In the distance he could see oil derricks and he told himself: Somewhere out there is an oil field with my name on it, it's just a matter of finding it.

The eternal dream of all adventurers.

After all, what was life but an adventure? If you played for high stakes you had to take chances.

It sounded great being land man for Stanolind, it was a prestige company, but it hadn't taken him long to realize that he could never go much beyond his salary of ten thousand a year there.

If you hit the right oil field you could make a couple million.

How he'd like to go back and flaunt that in Roberto Carvalho's face! Uncle Roberto. The thought of his stepfather made him choke with rage. For him his mother had abandoned all of them, for the caresses of that Brazilian bastard. . . .

Now he was sounding exactly like his father.

But he would love to see the expression on Carvalho's face when he became a successful oil man.

It was worth any price he had to pay.

He looked in the car mirror. The same green Chevy had been following him ever since he left the outskirts of town. The road now was deserted. He wondered whether to slow down and let him pass. He remembered the revolver he usually carried was locked in his desk at the office. He glanced in the mirror again. This was the same road where he'd had the accident that turned out not to be an accident.

The man honked his horn. He wanted to pass. Peter slowed down and the Chevy zoomed by, spraying more dirt on Peter's car.

He wasn't tailing me after all, Peter thought. I'm just getting edgy.

Billie's warning had upset him more than he wanted to let on to her. There'd been too many attempts for comfort lately. If Ruth Ellen knew she'd be worried sick. He felt guilty thinking of the hour he had just spent with Billie. He should have known what would happen if they got together.

But then they were both adults and they knew it was just for kicks.

Why was it that Ruth Ellen bored him to distraction? She was pretty and sweet and she adored him. . . .

He never should have married her. Well it was too late now to think of that. He was married to her and she was having his child.

There were times when he thought he should have just gone off and joined the French Foreign Legion.

A jackrabbit ran across the road and he swerved the car suddenly to avoid hitting him.

He had had a rabbit once when he was a little boy, a white rabbit with pink eyes and he had named him Pierre. One day he went in the rabbit hutch with a carrot to feed him and Pierre was dead. He had cried for weeks.

Did he care more for animals than he did for people? Sometimes he wondered.

The road now had turned into a cowpath leading into the oil fields.

There was a tract he wanted to check out, a mile of undrilled land next to one of the Humble oil fields. They said if you wanted to find oil get close to oil, and the leases on this tract were about to expire. Only trouble was these old ranchers were getting tougher and tougher to deal with. They had really smartened up about the oil business. Time was when you could buy land from them for practically nothing. Now they wanted part of the royalties as well.

A blue pickup truck was parked near a wooden shack and a man sitting in it munching on a sandwich eyed Peter with suspicion.

Companies were always raiding others looking for top-flight drilling foremen and geologists. It was part of the game.

Peter looked around. A drilling crew was lowering pipe into a hole. They had tough faces, splattered with mud and grease, and the armpits of their shirts were stained with sweat. They moved with precision in the broiling sun. Like a chain gang, Peter thought.

He drove past the row of oil derricks to the northeast edge of the field and then looked at his map again. Yes, this was where it began. His oil field.

He just had to buy up those leases somehow.

Already he could see his drilling rigs on the field and oil shooting up into the air.

All he needed was luck.

He got out of the car and walked around, surveying the property.

Suddenly he heard something stirring in a clump of mesquite bushes behind him. It stopped, then there was an unmistakable rattling sound and he stepped back quickly, looking at the same time for a large stick. A rattlesnake was coiled, ready to strike. He picked up a rock and threw it. The snake disappeared into the mesquite.

Was it some kind of omen? Peter wondered.

He got in his car and started the engine. He would go by the Petroleum Club, have a drink or two, ask a few questions.

The car stalled. It hadn't been acting right lately, he'd have to take it in to the garage as soon as he had a chance and have them go over it. He tried again. Damn, he must have flooded the engine. Now he'd have to sit here for a while until it cooled off.

This certainly wasn't his day.

A man was walking toward him. Peter recognized him as the one who'd been sitting in the blue pickup truck.

"Are you in trouble?" he asked.

"I think I've flooded it," Peter said.

"Want me to give you a push with my truck?"

There was something familiar about the man but Peter couldn't place where he'd seen him before. "Thanks," he said, "but I think I can get it going."

"Well if you can't, jest give a holler." He pointed to a thermos. "Like a cup of java?"

Peter didn't really want coffee but he was afraid the man would be offended if he refused.

"Thanks. That's very nice of you."

"Got plenty." The man poured two cups. "That one's gonna be a bitch-kitty," he said, nodding in the direction of the well.

"How far down are they?"

"Ten thousand feet. Should be blowing pretty strong."

"Have they been drilling long?"

"Two months."

"Well, I'll try again," Peter said, handing the man the empty cup. He turned the ignition key and the motor started. "I think it's all right now. Thanks for your help." He stepped hard on the accelerator and the car took off. He waved to the man.

As the car bumped over the rough road Peter glanced in his rear-view mirror. The man was still standing there and then Peter saw that he was writing something down on a piece of paper.

THREE

*H*e drove on. The road was a concrete ribbon running through the barren landscape, the dust hung thick, clogging the air. An oil supply truck passed going in the opposite direction.

He turned on the radio. A weather report. Present temperature one hundred and ten degrees. Thundershowers expected by evening.

It was three o'clock now and there was no indication of rain, but storms could come up suddenly here.

The car was heating up, he'd better pull into the first service station and put some water in the radiator. He glanced at the dashboard. The indicator needle registered hot.

In the distance he saw a Standard station. If he could just make it before the radiator boiled over. . . .

Funny, he was sure he'd had it filled only two days ago.

The engine was sputtering. "Easy, boy," he said. He felt like a pilot nursing a crippled plane.

He loved flying. He'd never gotten over the disappointment of being turned down by the Air Force during the war. As a boy he had read *Night Flight* by Antoine de Saint-Exupéry and determined to become a pilot. The battle with the elements, the soaring into the strange unknown appealed to him. When he heard that Saint-Exupéry had disappeared over the Alps on an Allied reconnaissance mission, he felt a sense of personal loss. His boyhood hero was gone.

Ah, but what a way to die! Peter thought. To vanish into the blue, to become part of the stars, the clouds. . . .

A hero's death.

Not the death of an old man, the slow withering of limbs, the dimming vision, the feeble steps, leaning on a cane, stooped, bent, saliva drooling, teeth decaying. He shuddered at the thought. We all grow old, some day he would be like that.

No, he could not picture it. He could not see himself old. Ever.

He would rather live with danger, take chances as Saint-Exupéry did.

The oil business was not quite the same as aviation but it was no game for pantywaists either. You had to be tough and yet have an air of nonchalance. People judged you on your own merits. No one gave a damn who your father was . . . or your grandfather.

Was it precisely this that had drawn him to Midland? The needing to prove himself as a man?

Yet he had not been able to understand the same feelings in a woman. But a woman was different, she was not meant to be independent, she was part of a man's life, she took his name and lived where he chose.

Valerie had not been willing to do that.

He could not get her out of his mind, no matter how hard he tried. The way she walked, golden hair spilling over violet eyes. . . .

There had been other women like Billie, ones who had physical appeal for the moment, and then you never wanted to see them again.

And Ruth Ellen, nice but unexciting, who deserved more than he would ever be able to give her.

You never marry the person you really want. Who had said that to him once?

It occurred to him that Valerie was in many ways very much like his mother.

"Who's that?" one of the boys at Andover had asked, pointing to the picture on his school bureau.

"My mother."

"Oh, come on."

"It is."

"If you say so."

The picture had been taken by Bachrach for *The Washington Post* in connection with a charity ball.

"If it's your mother how come she never visits the school?"

He had wanted to hit that boy. How could he explain about his mother and Uncle Roberto, how she didn't like to even admit she had a fifteen-year-old son? The beautiful Senhora Carvalho, who never sent him cookies like other mothers, who never showed up at school functions, who was only concerned that he got good marks and wasn't a bother.

"Bug off," he told the boy, "or I'll sock you."

At fifteen he was tall and skinny and his face was covered with acne. He was very self-conscious about it and tried every known remedy without success. Finally it cleared up by itself.

His father used to visit occasionally and would seek out his teachers and have hearty conversations with them. One time his father came up to school with some dame who looked like a chorus girl. At least he had the good sense to leave her in the car, but the guys could see her sitting there swathed in silver fox and they teased him about her later.

"Who was the platinum blonde with your dad?"

The memory still made him cringe.

He pulled into the Standard station. The car was smoking and an attendant came running up and lifted the hood.

"You've got trouble here, buddy."

"What is it?" Peter had gotten out of the car.

"See this?" The attendant pointed. "See that hole? Water just runs out as fast as you put it in. Looks to me like someone's been tampering with your car."

"How long would it take to repair it?"

"Well. . . ." The attendant scratched his head. "We could fix it up in about an hour, but that would just be temporary, get the point? You'd better take it into your dealer as soon as you can and have them replace the part. Is it still under warranty?"

"I'm not sure," Peter said. "You do what you can now. Do you have a Coke machine?"

"Right over there."

"Thanks."

Peter walked over and got a Coke. He'd take the car to the Ford dealer the first thing in the morning.

Who could have been tampering with it? Was it while he was in Billie's apartment? Or at the parking lot earlier? He had no way of knowing.

But one thing was sure. Whoever it was who was after him meant business.

Death was something that you think a lot about in war when you see other guys get it. You know it may happen to you too, and in a way you accept it. You become a fatalist. But this . . . having one person stalking you . . . was different. Or maybe there was more than one. It was like waiting for something to strike you out of the dark.

He must remember to go by the office and get his gun out of his desk. Not that that would do much good if he was taken by surprise. . . .

Billie hadn't been much help. If she knew, she wasn't telling. It was just a trick to get him to her place. Well he was through with that dame. He was going to try to be a decent husband to Ruth Ellen and a good father to their child.

Life was a series of compromises anyway. You never got everything you wanted.

He finished the Coke and put the empty bottle in the wire rack.

What would happen next? he wondered. A bomb wired so that when he stepped on the gas pedal the whole car blew up?

Last night he had had a dream, a terrible dream. . . .

He was in uniform lying on a battlefield with shells bursting all around him. He tried to call for help but he was bleeding from the throat, choking on his own blood.

Then the scene changed and he was in an ancient castle on the Rhine that had been converted to a hospital. He lay on a narrow cot in a large hall filled with wounded soldiers. There was a bandage on his throat.

Voices speaking in German buzzed around him. Through an open archway he could see rain pouring down and there was heavy thunder and lightning.

Then a soldier was brought in and put on the cot next to him. He had a blood-soaked bandage over one eye. With horror he recognized his former roommate, Dave Creighton.

"I got the bullet meant for you, Peter," he said.

"Dave, Dave, I'm sorry," he wanted to say, but he couldn't speak.

On the castle wall was a large oil painting of Hitler and a Nazi flag. Wide stone stairs led to a balcony and rooms from which he could hear laughter. Then a door opened and out came an officer wearing the S.S. tunic and breeches. He had his arms around two nude women.

"*Herr Obergruppenführer,*" someone said, "there are not enough beds for all the wounded."

"Then put them on the floor." He opened a bottle of iced Dom Perignon and poured it over one of the nude women. She ran giggling up the stairs. He took another bottle out of the ice bucket and started to untwist the metal cap seal.

One of the wounded soldiers was calling for water.

"No water," said a nurse. "He has a stomach wound."

The champagne bottle opened with a loud pop. The cork landed next to Peter's cot.

The S.S. officer walked over and looked down at the cot with a cruel smile. No wonder he looked familiar ... it was Roberto Carvalho.

"Uncle Roberto," Peter whispered. "What are you doing here? Where's Mother?"

"Nurse Schmidt," he called, snapping his fingers.

A nurse wearing a Swastika armband appeared. She had a plain scrubbed face and braided gray hair and Peter saw that it was Fräulein, his old nurse.

"*Ja, Herr Obergruppenführer?*"

"Put him on the floor." He took out a gold Dunhill lighter with the initials L.S. and lit a cigarette.

L.S. That's my father's lighter, Peter thought. "What are you doing with my father's lighter, you bastard!" he wanted to say, but the only sound that came from his bandaged throat was a hoarse croaking.

Fräulein was looking at him with pity, the way she used to when he was a little boy and had asthma attacks.

"He is choking," she said.

"We need this bed for German officers, you understand, Nurse Schmidt?"

"*Ja, Herr Obergruppenführer.*"

"*Er stirbt,*" he said, flicking ashes on Peter. His German had a strong Portuguese accent.

"I am not dying! I am not dying!" Peter woke, drenched with perspiration, to find Ruth Ellen standing over him.

"What's the matter, honey? You must have been having a terrible nightmare. You were waving your arms around and yelling something. What is it?"

"Nothing," he said. "Nothing." It had all seemed so real.

Now, he wondered if it had been more than a dream. Was it another warning?

And if so, what could he do about it?

He walked back to where they were working on his car.

FOUR

*H*is beagle came running out to greet him wagging his long brown-and-white tail.

"Hi, Tornado," Peter said, patting him. "Good boy."

Tornado jumped up and licked Peter's face.

"All right, I'm home now. That's enough. Down!"

In the kitchen Ruth Ellen was dipping pieces of chicken in a bowl of milk and coating them with flour. He walked over and kissed her on the cheek and wondered if she could smell any of Billie's perfume.

"Hello, honey." She looked hot and tired. "Did you have a good day?"

"Oh, so-so." He opened the refrigerator and took out a beer. "The car's been acting up again. I'll have to take it in tomorrow and have it checked."

"What's wrong with it?"

"Who knows?" He decided not to worry her. "I don't think it's anything serious. Any calls?"

"There was one about half an hour ago but when I answered they hung up." She took the black iron frying pan from a cupboard and put it on the stove. "Were you expecting something important?"

"Possibly."

Just then the phone rang.

"I'll get it," Peter said.

He walked into the living room and picked up the receiver. "Hello . . . hello . . . ." He waited. He knew there was someone on the line because he could hear breathing and he was starting to say "hello" for the third time when there was a sharp click.

"Who is it, honey?" Ruth Ellen called from the kitchen.

"Must be a wrong number. They hung up."

"There've been a lot of wrong numbers lately."

"Oh?" He wondered if Ruth Ellen knew more than she was saying.

"Yes, there was one this morning after you went to work. And last night when you were at that meeting. You'd think people would have the manners to say they're sorry instead of just banging down the phone."

Billie. That's who it must have been. She should have better sense than to call him at home. Damn that dame! he thought. "Has the paper come yet?" he asked.

"It should be here now."

"I'll get it." He opened the front door and saw the folded newspaper lying on the sidewalk. Not that there's much news in it, he thought, picking it up. The *Midland Reporter-Telegram* was not exactly *The New York Times*.

Ruth Ellen came out of the kitchen wiping her hands on an apron.

"The new Doris Day picture is opening tomorrow. Would you like to see it?" she asked.

"All right." He handed her the movie section and sat down on the couch. She sank down wearily beside him and rubbed her swollen ankles.

"I feel as if I'd been pregnant forever."

"It won't be long now."

"No. Just five more weeks." She sighed. "We still haven't decided on a name for a girl."

"It'll be a boy."

She laughed and the dimples showed in her cheeks. "Every father thinks that. Mine did."

"Oh, by the way, Chet Garrison asked about you today. Said to say hello and that they missed you."

She looked pleased. "That was nice of him."

"I think he'd like you back after the baby comes. Your replacement isn't as efficient."

"I'll be too busy. I'd like a big family, wouldn't you?"

"I guess."

"It's awful being an only child."

He stood up. "I think I'll take a shower before dinner."

There was a rumble of thunder in the distance and heat lightning streaked across the sky. Good, he thought, for once the weather bureau was right.

Another clap of thunder followed, closer this time.

In the back yard Tornado started to howl.

"I'll let him in," Ruth Ellen said.

Peter went in the bathroom and turned on the shower full force. He couldn't stand Ruth Ellen watching him with that look of patient understanding, that "you'll tell me when you want to" look. It would be better if she yelled at him and picked a fight. No, that wasn't really what he wanted, though it was what most women would do. He felt guilty as hell. Here she was, fixing his favorite dinner in this heat, while he . . . .

He lathered himself with soap and let the water run over his body. The scratches from Billie's nails had turned red, she had really dug into him. That dame was like a wildcat.

He grabbed a towel and the scratches stung as he rubbed his back.

That's what they all tried to do, make a claim on you.

"Dinner is almost ready, honey," Ruth Ellen called.

"All right."

He was a selfish bastard not to appreciate Ruth Ellen more, he told himself. She was pretty and sweet and she loved him, she would do anything for him, but she bored him to distraction.

You cannot make someone love you.

He took a pair of clean shorts from the bureau drawer.

"Women like men who treat them rough," his father said. Were men the same way, did they really prefer women who were mean to them to the devoted slaves? he wondered. His mother had treated his father like dirt and yet he still loved her. Perhaps there was some truth in it.

He put on a cotton shirt and a pair of slacks.

Ruth Ellen appeared at the bedroom door. "You look nice and cool," she said.

"I feel better. Dinner ready?"

"I'm just about to put it on the table."

I'm married to her. I'm stuck with her the rest of my life, he thought.

"I made you a lemon meringue pie."

"You shouldn't have gone to all that trouble."

"It's no trouble."

Had his mother ever baked pies for his father? He doubted it.

"I love to cook for you," she said.

He'd heard of servicemen who married Japanese wives and then became bored with them afterward. What made him think of that?

"I'd like another beer," he said.

"I'll get you one."

They sat down and she brought in the salad and fried chicken and corn.

The rain had started. It was coming down hard now, he could hear it beating on the roof and running down the gutters

"It's a regular cloudburst," Ruth Ellen said.

Another roll of thunder and more lightning.

There was a line of Hemingway's, "I see myself dead in the

rain," or something like that. It was from *A Farewell to Arms*. Was it the heroine who said that? Yes, when she was having the baby.

"Aren't you hungry, honey?"

"Oh . . . yes."

Ruth Ellen was studying him. "Something's bothering you."

Here it came. She wasn't that different from other women after all.

"No, not really." He picked up a chicken leg. "You sure know how to fix this."

"It's dipping it in sweet milk that's the trick. My mother taught me."

He tried to picture his own mother in a kitchen with flour-coated hands frying chicken, but he could only see her in a Dior gown and emeralds, every hair in place, the scent of carnations trailing her wherever she went. Was it possible for one woman to be everything?

"I'll get the pie," Ruth Ellen said.

"Would you save my piece till later?"

"Oh . . . all right."

She looked hurt. Damn, was it his fault if he wasn't hungry?

"Look, just cut me a small piece." He'd try and eat some.

She beamed. "You don't need to worry about your weight. I'm always trying to fatten you up and you never gain an ounce." She patted her stomach. "I guess I'll be thin again after the baby comes. I've almost forgotten what it's like."

After the baby comes. Would things be better between them then? he wondered. They said a child brought people closer together. But what if it didn't?

She put the pie in front of him and sat down again.

"You still haven't helped me with a girl's name. I think the father should choose it."

Did that mean she wanted the baby named after her? He thought of some of the names of women. Nina, his mother. No. His sister, Marcia. He didn't like that name either, even though they had always been very close. Besides, it was confusing naming a child after a living relative. And the way Southerners chose those damned double names. . . .

"We'll think of something," he said

"Do you think your mother will come out when the baby's born?" Ruth Ellen asked. "I'd love to meet her."

No, he didn't think so. "Maybe," he said. "Brazil's a long way off."

"I know. I wish we'd hear from her more often."

He pushed the pie away. "It's delicious, but that's all I can eat now. Put it in the refrigerator for me and I'll finish it later."

He walked over to the window and watched the rain beat on the parched earth. It seemed nothing would grow here in this stubborn soil. He had tried to plant a few flowers but just as they were coming up a sandstorm buried them. At least his son wouldn't have to worry about having a sandpile in his back yard. Just give him a pail and shovel and let him think he was at the beach. He looked at the half-finished cement-block wall he had started to build around his yard as one of his weekend projects. All his neighbors had them and it helped to keep out the sand drifts, they said. The houses all looked alike—like a colony of ant hills, he thought.

And we are the ants looking for oil, digging, burrowing into the ground, hoping to strike it rich so we can take our pile and move away from here. Only the old ranching families stayed on in Midland for more than one generation.

He sat down on the sofa and started to read the latest copy of the *Oil and Gas Journal*. Tornado lay at his feet.

The sky darkened, yet the rain continued.

"Looks like it's going to rain all night," Ruth Ellen said. "We can certainly use a good soaking."

He felt restless. He wanted to go for a walk . . . anywhere. The hall clock chimed nine.

Suddenly Tornado sat up and gave a low growl. Peter reached down and stroked him.

"Ssh, boy," he said. "It's all right."

Tornado listened for a minute and then the hair on his body stood on end.

"He hears something," Ruth Ellen said.

They could hear nothing but the sound of the rain. The dog continued to growl and ran to the doors and windows.

"I'd better check," Peter said. "You stay in the house and keep the door closed."

"Be careful ... it could be a prowler." Ruth Ellen looked frightened.

"Go into the bedroom," he said, "and stay there."

Damn, he'd meant to go by the office and get his gun.

Cautiously he opened the front door and looked around. The street was deserted. He started to walk toward the sidewalk and suddenly he felt cold steel hitting his left temple and blood ran down his face into his eyes, he could taste it in his mouth, someone was holding him from behind, there was a piercing pain and he heard the dull thud of a revolver butt pounding his head and he tried to struggle and couldn't. He fell to his knees in the mud. The brown soil was streaked with red and blood continued to pour from the open cut on his forehead, he felt weak and nauseated, and then he was flung over on his back and a flash of lightning illuminated the face of the person standing above him and he saw the gun pointed at his chest.

There was a loud explosion and then all went black. . . .

FIVE

*I*n the bedroom Ruth Ellen waited. Tornado licked her hand and whimpered. "It's all right," she said, patting him. "He'll be right back." Tornado hated storms. They had found him after one of the spring tornadoes huddled on their front doorstep, shivering and bedraggled. "I wonder who he belongs to, poor little hound," Peter said. The dog had no collar and gobbled down the food they gave him. "I don't think he's eaten in days," Peter said, watching him. "Don't worry, boy, we'll take care of you." They never found his owner and so he remained with them.

Tornado was running in circles with his tail between his legs giving strange little moaning sounds. Peter should be back by now, she thought. Suddenly she could stand it no longer. She ran to the front door and flung it open and then she let out a piercing scream.

He was lying sprawled on the sidewalk in a pool of blood.

"Peter!"

She threw herself down beside him in the rain. There was a jagged cut on his forehead and his face was battered and bruised. Dark blood oozed from wounds in his chest.

"Someone . . . help!"

She cradled his head in her lap and tried to wipe away the blood with her skirt. "Peter . . . Peter!" Over and over again she kept calling his name, as if, by doing so, she could bring him back to life.

And that was the last she remembered.

✤

"I reckon somebody was sure out to get him."

"Yeah. A handsome guy, or was. Too bad."

"Ssh, she's coming to."

She was lying on the sofa with a cold cloth on her forehead and the house was filled with people. Her neighbors were there and her doctor and a man with a silver star on a rawhide vest—she had seen him somewhere before. He was about fifty and his black hair was salted with gray and his face was tan and leathery, but his eyes were kind.

"I'm Sheriff Mahoney, ma'am."

Oh. The sheriff.

"I'm sorry, but I reckon I'm going to have to ask you some questions."

She stared at him numbly.

"Do you have any idea who would have wanted to kill your husband?"

She shook her head. "No, I. . . ." Across the room a man with a camera was making notes.

"He never told you about the other attempts on his life?"

"Other attempts?" She tried to sit up. They must have given her some kind of sedative. She felt groggy. Tears started to run down her cheeks. This wasn't a nightmare after all, it was real. She began to sob.

"I don't think she's up to any questioning yet, Sheriff. She's still in shock." It was Doc Kelsey's voice.

There was a blinding flash from the camera and she screamed in terror.

"Get that reporter out of here," the sheriff ordered. "Now,

ma'am," his gruff voice sounded almost gentle, "we need your help."

She continued to stare at him. Help? she thought. How can I help when everything is finished? It's all over. Nothing can bring Peter back to me now. Why must you ask me these questions? What does anything matter now?

"You don't know of anyone who might have had a grudge against your husband?"

"My husband had no enemies. Everyone liked him."

"I'm not trying to imply anything, ma'am. We're just trying to find a motive. Whoever it was who did it had a very strong reason." He paused. "I'm sorry to have to ask you this, but was your marriage happy?"

"Yes." She stiffened. What was he getting at?

"And had you known your husband long when you married him?"

Long? What was long? Time did not matter. It was possible to know in an instant whether you could love someone or not, and she had fallen in love with Peter the first day she saw him.

The sheriff repeated his question.

"About a year," she said.

"You were a secretary at the Stanolind Oil Company then?"

She nodded, and the questions continued, and she answered like a mechanical doll that you wind up, feeling nothing but emptiness, and she dreaded that presently she would come back to life and feel again, and she would not be able to bear the pain. By talking about him they could make him live again, and she could go back in her mind and see him, not the way she had last seen him lying there dead in the rain, but the way he looked on the day she met him, that day he came to work for the Stanolind Oil Company. . . .

She was sitting at her desk in the outer office when Judy at the next desk nudged her and said, "Get a load of the cute Yalie."

That was the term they used for all the Ivy League boys who had come to Midland since the end of the war. It wasn't hard to tell them from the local Texans and this one was no exception, except that he was better looking. He was wearing a blue cotton cord suit with a white button-down shirt and narrow striped tie and tan loafers. She smiled to herself. He'd change those clothes pretty quick out here.

He was coming toward her. His hair was dark brown and slicked back and she noticed how blue his eyes were.

"I have an appointment with Mr. Garrison at eleven," he said. His voice was low and had a definite Eastern accent.

"I'll tell him you're here, Mister. . . ."

"Spaulding. Peter Spaulding."

She buzzed on the intercom. "Mr. Garrison, Peter Spaulding is here to see you. . . . Yes, I'll tell him."

He was adjusting his tie and she thought, He's nervous. There was none of the brash Texan about him.

"Mr. Garrison will see you now, Mr. Spaulding. Right through that door." She pointed and smiled.

"Thank you very much." He smiled back, a half-shy smile and was gone. She was on her lunch hour when he came out and she wondered what had happened to him. Was he a new employee or was he seeing Mr. Garrison about an oil deal? She kept waiting for him to come in the office again. She found out he had been hired by the company as an oil lease man and was working out in the fields. The other girls were curious about him too. "I hear he's from a society family back East," one of them said. "Gee, I'd sure like to get a date with him. He's real good-looking."

And then two weeks later she saw him.

At first she almost didn't recognize him. He was wearing Levi's and boots and a sports shirt and he had a deep tan. He came up to her desk and smiled. "Good morning. Is Mr. Garrison busy?"

"I'll see." She checked and found that he was on a long distance phone call. "Won't you sit down and wait? I'm sure he'll be through soon."

"Thanks." He sat down in a chair near her desk.

"You look different," she said.

"Oh, yes." He smiled. "These clothes are more comfortable. But nothing keeps out the heat. How do you stand it?"

She laughed. "You'll get used to it."

"Are you from Midland?"

"Fort Worth. But I've been living here for two years."

"So you're a native Texan?"

"Yes. I've never been out of Texas."

He looked surprised and then he said, "Well, I guess you can go a long way around here without getting out of Texas."

The buzzer flashed and she picked up the phone. "Mr. Garrison will see you now," she said.

"Good." He smiled at her and went in the office.

She retyped the letter she had been doing and started another but her fingers kept hitting all the wrong keys. Don't be silly, she told herself. He doesn't even know you're alive.

She would skip her lunch if necessary to be sure she was here when he came out. She waited. Maybe he would ask her to have lunch with him.

After ten minutes he came out of Mr. Garrison's office and scarcely nodding in her direction, walked through the front door. Later, she would remember that he looked worried.

Her gaze fell on the silver star of Sheriff Mahoney and she was brought back to the present.

He was asking her something about her family.

"I don't have any family," she said. It was then that she realized who Sheriff Mahoney reminded her of. Her father. How proud she was of him. "My daddy's a Texas Ranger," she used to tell her classmates. And then there was that awful day when she was ten and she was brought home from school and told that her daddy was dead. He was shot by a bandit fleeing in a stolen car. Things were never the same after that. Her mother went to work in a grocery store and Ruth Ellen would come home from school to an empty house. Often her mother, exhausted from standing on her feet all day, was too weary to do more than open a can of soup for supper, so Ruth Ellen took over the cooking and housework.

The years passed. She graduated from high school during the war, and then her mother died of cancer and she was all alone. She took a secretarial course and one day she saw an ad in the newspaper that there were good-paying secretarial jobs to be had in Midland, much better than in Fort Worth or Dallas. When she first saw Midland she understood why they were offering higher salaries to come there. She took an apartment with another girl and they both wondered where all the single men were that they expected to find in Midland. She discovered that most of the men who came to work for the oil companies also brought their wives.

But Peter Spaulding wasn't married, that much she had found out. She wondered if he had a girl back home.

She ran into him several days later in the Scharbauer Hotel coffee shop. He was sitting at the white marble counter drinking iced tea and reading the newspaper and there was an empty place beside him. She slid into it.

He turned around and gave her a smile of recognition. "Hello," he said. "How are you?"

"Fine." She smiled brightly, glad that she had on one of her most becoming cotton dresses and had washed her hair the night before. She almost hadn't. "How's everything going?"

"Oh, pretty good."

"We haven't seen you in the office the last few days."

"I've been in Odessa trying to tie up an oil lease." He glanced toward the lobby as if he were expecting someone, then back at her.

The Scharbauer Hotel lobby was where most of the business in Midland was transacted. Ranchers and lease brokers and oil company scouts drifted in and out of the lobby, talking in groups and unrolling maps. It was hard to tell the millionaires from the cowhands because they all dressed in the same wrinkled, shabby clothes.

Peter went back to his newspaper again. The waitress came over and Ruth Ellen ordered a tuna on rye and iced coffee. There was a slight breeze from the ceiling fans that turned slowly overhead. She wondered how to get a conversation started again. "Have you seen the rodeo?" she asked.

"No, I haven't."

"It's the big event around here every summer—it lasts four days and they have roping and all the best cowboys from Texas and New Mexico." She wondered if she was being too bold and if he would think that she was hinting he take her. "It's really something to see."

"Good. I may stop by and take a look at it. It goes on for four days you say?"

She nodded. "Do you ride?"

"I used to, but I haven't been on a horse since I got out of the Army." He looked toward the lobby again and then saw the person he was waiting for. The man was husky with a ruddy complexion and wore faded blue cowboy trousers, a wide leather belt with a large silver buckle, Western boots, and a wildly-figured sports shirt. He was holding a rolled-up map.

Peter put some money on the counter and got up. "Goodbye. Have a nice day," he said, and was gone.

Darn, I'm not getting anywhere with him, she thought. He didn't even know her name and he hadn't asked. She finished her sandwich and went back to the office.

"I know how difficult this is for you, ma'am, but can you think of anything that seemed strange about your husband's behavior?"

Dimly she heard the sheriff's voice. Why must he keep on and on with these questions? She wanted to scream: Everyone go out and leave me alone! Leave me alone! I don't know anything. I only know that Peter is dead and I will never see him again. She started to sob and Doc Kelsey came over and said, "Sheriff, I don't think she can take any more right now. I'd like to give her a sedative so she can sleep"

Sleep. Yes, sleep . . . endlessly, she thought.

Sheriff Mahoney stood up. "I'll come back tomorrow," he said. "Has that call gotten through to Rio de Janeiro?"

"We're still trying."

SIX

"*S*enhora Carvalho—é muito importante!"

Maria, her Brazilian maid, was excited and spoke so rapidly that even though Nina understood Portuguese, she had difficulty making out what Maria was trying to tell her.

"*Fale mais devagar, Maria,*" Nina said. She had just walked into her apartment after luncheon with friends at the Gavea Golf Club. It was a beautiful afternoon and on the drive home she thought again how much she loved Rio de Janeiro. They had lived here nearly two years now, ever since Roberto retired from the diplomatic corps.

Maria handed her a message. "*Muito importante,*" she repeated.

"*Obrigada.*" Nina looked at the number. She was to call the overseas operator. An urgent call from Midland, Texas.

I wonder what it can be? she thought. Could the baby have arrived early? It wasn't due until August.

She still could not accept the idea of being a grandmother. And why did Peter have to marry that little nobody from Texas, a secretary or something, when he could have had his pick of the Washington debutantes? She couldn't believe it when he had written and said he was married.

Nina went into her bedroom and took off her wide-brimmed

hat. She was always careful to protect her white complexion from the strong Brazilian sun. Besides, sun made lines in a woman's face. Let those young girls get a tan like burnt toast if they wanted. They'd pay for it at forty. She studied herself in the mirror. She had passed that terrible dividing line six years ago, but her face was still unlined, and with her blue-green almond-shaped eyes and black hair and slim figure she could pass for thirty. Well, thirty-five at most, she told herself. She'd have to take a nap before the dinner party tonight at the American Embassy.

She sat down on the four-poster bed of ornately carved jacarandá with its pale green silk canopy and asked the overseas operator to try the call to Midland. Roberto would be home any minute and if it was any kind of a problem she didn't want him to know about it. He always became so irritated over anything concerning her children.

Why could she not have seen this quality in him before she married him? But it wouldn't have mattered. She would have married him anyway.

They were having trouble getting through to Midland. She lay back on the bed and kicked off her high-heeled pumps, admiring her legs as she did so. Too bad skirts almost to the ankle were fashionable now. She'd been furious at Dior ever since he introduced the New Look two years ago. Of course, skirts did get a little short during the war, but these were ridiculous. From one extreme to the other. She opened a box covered in iridescent butterfly wings and took out a gold-tipped cigarette.

What is taking them so long? she wondered.

Finally, after an endless delay, she heard the unmistakable twang of the Texas operator, and she waited to hear Peter's voice, but the operator interrupted.

"Is this Senhora ... Carval-ho?" She gave the "h" the hard sound instead of the Portuguese "yo."

"Yes, this is Senhora Carvalho speaking." These stupid Texans, they had probably never even heard of Brazil. For them nothing existed outside of Texas. Why did Peter want to live there? "Peter . . . is that you, darling?"

"Ma'am?" It was a man's voice, gruff, with a heavy drawl. "This is Sheriff Mahoney, ma'am."

Sheriff. Why would a sheriff be calling? Unless Peter had been in an accident. The way those Texans drove. . . .

"I'm afraid there's bad news, ma'am."

She steeled herself for what was coming. The aquamarine bracelet that Roberto had given her for their anniversary felt like ice cutting into her wrist.

"My son?"

"Yes, ma'am."

Stop calling me "ma'am" and tell me what has happened, she wanted to scream. "A car accident?" There was no reply. "How badly is he hurt?"

"No, ma'am, it wasn't a car accident. It was a shooting."

"He's not. . . ." Slowly she grasped what he was trying to tell her and yet she could not bring herself to believe it. "He's not . . . dead?"

"I'm afraid so, ma'am." The gruff voice was gentle. "I'm sorry to have to break it to you this way."

"Oh, my God!"

She could hear the waves breaking on Copacabana Beach and she gripped the phone and the waves seemed to be sweeping over her. She was drowning and there was nothing to hang on to, no hand reaching out to pull her safely to shore. Through the French windows that opened onto the terrace she could see Sugar Loaf and the islands in the bay outlined against a mauve sky and she thought how unreal it all seemed, this strange Texas sheriff on the phone telling her that her son had been shot. He had gone through the war without a scratch, he had been cited for bravery on the battlefields of Italy, she had a letter from General Mark Clark telling her of his heroism. And then he had gone on to France and the liberation of Paris, he had escaped the snipers' bullets and returned home safely. He had been killed, instead, in Texas.

"How did it happen?" It did not sound like her voice, but like that of a woman suddenly grown old.

"We don't rightly know, ma'am. I reckon it would be a good idea for you to come on here as soon as you can."

"Yes. Of course. I'll take the next plane."

Numbly, she put down the phone. She must compose herself and call the airport. She had to pack. The dinner party tonight. She must cancel it. No, Roberto could go alone. She rang for Maria. She mustn't go to pieces. Not yet. There was so much to do. Afterward. . . .

And then a scene flashed through her mind. It was when Peter was six, right after she had divorced Lathrop. She was sitting on the edge of Peter's bed listening to his prayers. He was wearing blue pajamas that matched his eyes and his dark hair was tousled and he looked like a Botticelli angel. His small hands were folded and he blessed everyone including his pet chipmunk and turtle, and when he had finished he opened his eyes and looked at her with a grave expression.

"You won't ever stop loving me, will you Mummy?" he asked.

"Of course not, darling. What a silly question!"

"I mean you won't stop loving me . . . the way you did Daddy?"

Lathrop Spaulding looked dully out the plane window waiting for the take-off, his trembling hands clutching an unread copy of *The New York Times*. He was glad the seat next to him was empty. He did not feel like talking to anyone.

Murder.

An ugly word, something you read about in newspapers, something that happened to other people, people you didn't know, strangers. My son, he thought. Why you?

He was a big man, six-foot-two and heavy set, his thick sandy hair streaked with gray and blue eyes that were red-rimmed and swollen under his dark glasses. Until last night, when they called him from Midland, he had not cried in a long time. Years, in fact. Since right after Nina left him. When he realized she was serious about a divorce and wanted to marry another man. "The beautiful Senhora Carvalho," the papers called her. Even seeing her name in print after all this time could still cause him pain. That bitch, he thought, and a muscle stood out on his forehead and his heart beat faster, and the dividing line between love and hate, that narrow line that separated his feelings for her vanished, and the past washed over him again and he knew that he was still in love with her and always would be.

There had been a lot of women since Nina, but none of them had erased the memory of her or even come close.

Nina. . . .

The plane started to taxi down the runway. He leaned back in his seat and closed his eyes. He was no longer aware of the present.

Warren Harding was President, Fred and Adele Astaire were dancing on Broadway, and Lathrop was a senior at Yale. It was at a prom that he first saw Nina. It was hard to miss seeing her. She was wearing a shimmering green dress and even across the room her beauty dazzled him. The stag line was giving her a rush.

"Nice, eh?" said Herb van Rensselaer.

"Who is she?"

"Nina McDonnell. She's from Baltimore."

"Who's she with?"

"Ted Reeves."

"How did he rate?"

Ted Reeves was short and chubby and hardly the kind who would appeal to girls, especially the vision in green. What Lathrop did not know then was that Nina McDonnell would have accepted an invitation from anyone to come to Yale. The band started to play the new dance rage, the Charleston.

"Why don't you cut in?" Herb asked.

"I'll wait for something slower." He noticed that she was an expert at the Charleston. She could have been a professional dancer, and he remembered the time one of the boys as a joke had brought a chorus girl to a prom and passed her off as a debutante. Nina McDonnell's legs in the green satin pumps were as good as the ones in any Broadway musical, and he wondered why so many of the girls from the so-called good families had "piano legs."

Which reminded him of his date, Sally Cunningham. He would have to cut back on her in a few minutes. Sally was from Long Island and had pale blonde hair, pale eyebrows and eyelashes, and pink skin that freckled in the sun. She was a nice girl and a good sport, but completely without sex appeal. He wondered why he had asked her to the prom, but he had just broken up with another girl and he didn't know whom to ask. He had to have a date and Sally was available.

The band switched to another number and he walked over and tapped the boy dancing with Nina McDonnell.

"Hello," he said. "I'm Lathrop Spaulding."

"Hello, Lathrop Spaulding." She gave him a dazzling smile.

"I hope you don't mind my cutting in. Ted's been talking about you so much I couldn't believe you were real. He's a lucky guy." This wasn't strictly true, in fact Ted had been very mysterious about the girl he was bringing and refused to divulge anything about her.

"Oh?" Her eyebrows went up, as if she wondered what Ted had been saying. Her eyes were blue-green and almond-shaped and framed in thick black lashes. Long pearl earrings dangled under her bobbed dark hair and her skin was like the carved ivory figurines his mother collected. "Ted's sweet," she said. "He's an old friend."

This was what he wanted to know. Now the coast was clear. She looked younger than he had thought at first, even though she was trying to appear very sophisticated. Sixteen, maybe? Seventeen at most.

"That's quite a Charleston you do," he said. "I was watching you from the sidelines."

"Oh, thank you."

"Maybe you'll teach me. I haven't learned it yet."

"All right. It's easy."

He felt a tap on his shoulder. "See you later," he said to Nina, and reluctantly went in search of Sally.

The stewardess was hooking a tray into his seat.

"I'm not hungry," he said.

"Nothing at all?" She looked disappointed.

"No. Thank you." I just want to be left alone, he thought. He was angry that she had interrupted his reverie. For a brief moment he had been able to recapture something that was gone. Now he was conscious again of the present. He felt all of his fifty years.

Nina. For a long time he had hoped that she would come back to him, saying that it had all been a mistake. Fool, he thought. Yet the hope would not die. It was always in his mind, a part of his life, dull and heavy, nudging him, other women meant nothing, Nina was always there. Every room had her scent, her laugh, a laugh that in the end became taunting, contemptuous, yet it was hers and belonged to no one else. He never walked down a street without hoping that he might find her at the end of it, walking toward him.

He lit a cigarette and his hands were still trembling. He must get hold of himself.

Who was to blame for what had happened? And now, Peter, their son. Murdered. It still did not seem real. How? Why? He dreaded the questions, the probing, the intimate details of their lives that would be spread across the tabloids for all to read.

Everything would come out now.

Nina. If they could share this together, comfort each other in their mutual grief. No, she did not need him, she had Carvalho. But Peter was not Carvalho's son, Carvalho hated him, Peter had told him so on his visits to Wynwood. Carvalho would not come to the funeral, Nina would come alone.

And they would meet again over the grave of their son.

SEVEN

Still drugged from sedatives and numb with shock, Ruth Ellen started to make the funeral arrangements. Peter had been raised as an Episcopalian, and while he seldom attended church, except Christmas and Easter, she felt he would have wanted an Episcopal funeral service. It was better to have everything settled before the members of his family arrived.

His father was on his way now from New York and would be here in a few hours, and his mother was taking the next plane from Rio de Janeiro. Marcia was finally reached on a ranch outside of Reno where she was establishing her six-weeks residency for divorce and would not be able to come.

She had never met any of his family and now she realized that he had told her very little about them. When she looked back it was strange how much there was that she didn't know. It was as if his life began when he came to Midland. As if he wanted to start anew and leave the past behind. From what was he fleeing? Or whom?

There had been other attempts on his life since he had been in Midland, the sheriff said. Why, then, had Peter never mentioned them to her? And why had he walked out of the house at night without a gun if he knew someone was after him? None of it made sense.

Unless he wanted to die. . . .

Was your marriage happy? the sheriff had asked her. She felt icy cold. Was there something he was getting at, something she didn't know? Did he suspect that another woman was involved? She thought of the mysterious telephone calls and how the caller always hung up when she answered.

She tried to think back, to go over the brief months of their marriage and the time she had known him before that. . . .

❖

She had despaired of Peter ever asking her for a date. They spoke when he came in the office and he was always very friendly, but that was as far as it went. He was obviously not interested, or else he had a girl back East somewhere. She decided to put him out of her mind.

And then she ran into him at a party some friends of hers were giving. She noticed he wasn't with anyone and she had come alone. He seemed pleased to see her and they found themselves in a corner of the room talking.

"Washington must be a fascinating place," she said.

He shrugged. "I guess so."

"Did you always live there?"

"No. . . I was born in New York. We moved to Washington when I was six. After my parents were divorced."

"Do you have any brothers or sisters?"

"A younger sister."

"Is she still in Washington?"

"Marcia? No, she's married and lives on Long Island."

"I always wanted a brother or sister. I was an only child and it was pretty lonely."

"Marcia and I were very close. Mother was always going out, so we didn't see too much of her when we were growing up." His voice had a bitter edge. "And it was better to stay out of my stepfather's way after we moved to the embassy."

"The embassy?"

"My stepfather was the Brazilian Ambassador. He'd been a bachelor all his life and children got on his nerves."

"That must have been hard on you."

"I wasn't there too much. I went away to boarding school, and my father had this place in Maryland and Marcia and I used to visit him during the summer. It was on an island in Chesapeake Bay and there was sailing and a lot of things to do."

"Does your father still live there?"

"No, he sold it during the war when my grandmother died. It was a pretty big place and it was hard getting servants."

It seemed to be a sore spot with him, she noticed.

"Where did you go to college?" she asked.

"I went to Princeton for two years, but then the war came and I enlisted in the Army. When it was over I didn't feel like going back and finishing. I suppose I should have."

"Most of the men in the oil business don't have college degrees."

"I've noticed that. Maybe one of these days I can po'boy me a well like Roy Gilmore over there."

Roy waved. "How y'doing?"

"Fine," Peter said.

"So I see." Roy walked over, chewing on an unlighted cigar. His silvery hair was parted in the middle and plastered down on both sides and he was wearing a rumpled tan gabardine suit, the coat open to display a huge belt buckle of diamonds. His tie clip had two diamonds and a ruby, and a diamond ring flashed on his left hand.

"How y'like my boots?" he asked, hitching up a trouser leg. They were of pink and blue leather stitched with gold thread and glittering with diamonds. "Had 'em made last week in San Antone. Designed 'em myself," he said proudly.

Peter gulped. "They're quite something."

"Yeah. Cost two hundred and fifty a pair. I've ordered me ten more pairs like 'em."

"Right smart-looking boots, Roy," someone called.

"Damned if they ain't," Roy chuckled. He slapped Peter on the back. "See you around, young feller." He smiled at Ruth Ellen. "Bring your girl to the barbecue at the ranch next Sunday."

"Thank you, sir."

Roy moved on.

"He's quite a character," Peter said. "Now, where were we?"

"You'd just gotten out of the Army."

"Oh, yes. Well, all that's pretty dull. Would you like to go to the barbecue? Unless you're busy or something."

"No . . . but he kind of put you on the spot. I'm not your girl . . . I mean perhaps there's someone else you'd rather take."

He shook his head. "I'd like you to go with me."

"Then I'd like to very much."

Roy Gilmore's ranch was between Midland and Odessa, set back from the main highway at the end of a winding road. The house was of rough-hewn stone and glass, and on either side of the front door was an elephant tusk set in concrete.

"Roy bagged him on a safari," Peter told Ruth Ellen. "Wait until you see the rest of the house. There's a lion's head that he shot in Kenya over the living room mantel and a polar bear rug in the master bedroom. Roy shot him in Alaska. He'll tell you all about each one if you give him half a chance. In fact, try and stop him," Peter laughed.

Roy was in the middle of the living room greeting guests. Peter and Ruth Ellen worked their way through the crowd.

"Hi, young feller," Roy said, pumping Peter's hand. "And you, little lady. Mighty nice to see you. The missus is around here someplace." He glanced around the room.

"That's all right, sir. We'll find her."

A man in a rumpled brown suit and orange boots called to Roy. "They finish your well yet?"

"Nope. Down to fourteen thousand feet. A couple more days." Roy turned back to Peter and Ruth Ellen. "Old Sam there just drilled his ninth dry hole in a row."

"That must be pretty discouraging," Peter said.

"Yeah. 'Dry-Hole Sam' they call him. Now me, I've been real lucky. Let me give you a tip, young feller. Luck is everything in this game, and don't let nobody ever tell you no different. You can be real smart and not be lucky. Remember that."

"I'll try, sir."

"Take Earl Copeland over there. . . ." He waved his hand in the direction of a husky, red-faced man who was busy talking to a group of people. "There's a lucky bastard. Always comes out with his nose clean, old Earl does. D'ya know him?"

"I've met him," Peter said, and suddenly Ruth Ellen remembered the man in the Scharbauer Hotel with the rolled-up map.

"Luck, my boy, luck. Some have it, some don't."

Just then a plump peroxide blonde came weaving across the room. She was wearing a blue shantung dress with two enormous sapphire clips and a diamond bracelet.

"There she is," Roy said "Daisy Belle, here are some folks I'd like you to meet. Peter Spaulding and—"

"This is Ruth Ellen Tyler," Peter said quickly.

"So happy you could come. Roy's been telling me about you, Mr. Spaulding. Aren't you the new geologist for Stanolind?"

"No, I negotiate oil-land leases for them. And please call me Peter."

"Then you must call me Daisy Belle." She turned to Ruth Ellen. "We're real informal here in Texas."

"Ruth Ellen's a native Texan," Peter said.

"Oh? Funny we've never met before."

"You've a lovely home," Ruth Ellen said.

"Why, thank you, dear."

"Say, did Peter tell you the story of those elephant tusks out front?" Roy asked. "I was on this safari in Africa and—"

"Oh come on, Roy, you're not going to tell that story again? We've all heard it a million times," Daisy Belle said with irritation.

"I'd love to hear it sometime, Mr. Gilmore," Ruth Ellen said.

"Yes, but this is not the time," said Daisy Belle.

"Peter tells me that you're quite an art connoisseur, Mrs. Gilmore," Ruth Ellen said.

"A what?"

"That you collect paintings."

"Oh, yes. Would you like to see some of them?" Daisy Belle patted a stray curl back in place. "I'll give you the tour. That's a Chagall over there—and a Modigliani. I can never pronounce his name," she giggled. "Say, did you folks get a drink?"

"We'll get one later," Peter said.

They were in the master bedroom. It was all done in white with touches of persimmon. A low antique cabinet next to the bed contained a bar.

"This fag decorator we had down from Los Angeles didn't want to put this in," Daisy Belle explained.

The bed was strewn with mink stoles, even though it was July. Ruth Ellen had never seen so many. She had brought a white linen coat. "Lay it in there, honey," Daisy Belle said. She opened a huge walk-in closet. "Got those in Paris. They're all designer originals. I always go to Paris and shop when Roy goes off on his safaris."

The bathroom had a sunken tub and a low kind of basin next to the toilet. Ruth Ellen had never seen anything like it before. She wondered what it was.

"That's a bidet," Daisy Belle said. "I had it shipped over from Paris. Only one in Midland."

Ruth Ellen noticed that Peter flushed slightly.

"It's real handy for soaking your feet too," Daisy Belle said. "That's what I told Roy when he complained about the price. Well, I'd better be getting back to my guests."

"Thank you for showing us everything, Mrs. Gilmore," Ruth Ellen said.

"Daisy Belle."

"Daisy Belle," Ruth Ellen repeated hesitantly.

"Now you folks just go get yourselves a drink and make yourselves to home." Daisy Belle glanced at herself in the mirror, frowned, and tugged at her girdle. "I've got to go on another diet. How do you stay so slim, honey?"

"Oh, I don't know."

"You're sure a little thing. Isn't she, Peter? I bet she don't weigh more than a hundred pounds stripped."

"About that," Ruth Ellen said.

"Roy says he likes his women with flesh on," Daisy Belle giggled, "but those Paris fashion designers sure don't agree."

Peter was standing in front of a collection of guns in a glass-doored case on the wall of Roy's dressing room.

"That's Roy's collection," Daisy Belle said. "Well, folks, look around if you'd like. I'd better get back to my other guests." Giving her girdle another tug, she was gone.

Peter laughed and shook his head. "What do you think of Daisy Belle?"

"I like her. She's warm and friendly. Do they have any children?"

"Not that I know of. Just a couple of race horses."

"It must be fun going to Paris to buy your clothes. Imagine, all designer originals! Have you ever been to Paris?"

"As a child, but I barely remember that. And at the end of the war. We went in with the Liberation."

"I'd love to go there."

They started toward the living room.

"You know one of the things I like about you?" Peter said suddenly. "You have so much enthusiasm about everything. Most of the girls I know in the East are so blasé. You're not."

"Oh?" She had often wondered about those girls and envied them.

"You seem . . . well, just happy to be alive. That must be great."

"I've never really thought about it before, but I guess I am happy most of the time. Aren't you?"

"No," he said. "I never have been."

She had tried to make him happy, and there were times when she thought he was. Almost. No, there was always something missing. Something she had never been able to supply. And she wondered if any woman could have made him happy.

She felt a sharp pain and she drew up her knees. She couldn't be going into labor now. It was too soon. She must stay calm for the baby's sake and not let anything upset her. The baby was all she had to live for now.

She clenched her fists as another pain came. Tears started to roll down her cheeks again. Somehow she could get through all this, she told herself. She could do what must be done.

Still, she felt so alone.

Sheriff Mahoney looked at the map of oil drillings on the wall and then back at Chet Garrison. "How would you describe Peter Spaulding?" he asked, watching Garrison's face carefully. The man seemed really upset by his employee's death, but then he'd seen cover-ups before.

"A quiet, likable chap. Not the kind you'd expect to end up murdered."

"Anything you can recall that might give us a clue as to why he was?"

Garrison hesitated, then shook his head "But there was one thing I thought odd."

"What was that?"

"The day before he was killed, two federal agents came in here and wanted to talk to me about him."

Sheriff Mahoney leaned forward. "Did they say why?"

"No. But they sure asked a lot of questions."

"Like what?"

"How he came to be hired, what I knew about his friends, his jobs before he worked for Stanolind. . . ."

"Did you mention that visit to Spaulding?"

"Yes, when he came in the office," Garrison said. "I had the feeling he was in some kind of trouble and I asked him if there was anything he wanted to level with me about."

"What did he say?"

"Nothing."

"I see. Not much to go on. His wife worked for you, didn't she?"

"Yes, for two years. A nice girl, Ruth Ellen. Pretty tough on her, expecting a baby so soon. I'd like to help in any way I can."

"If you can remember anything else that might shed some light on this case, let me know." The sheriff got up. "Do you have the name of those agents?"

"I think so." Garrison looked in his desk drawer for the card and handed it to the sheriff. "A tragic thing," he said.

"Thanks. I'll get in touch with them."

As he turned to walk to the door, Sheriff Mahoney was sure he saw tears in Garrison's eyes.

EIGHT

Y ears ago, when she had first married Roberto, Nina had learned to pack for sudden trips, how to fold her clothes in tissue paper so they came out with scarcely a wrinkle, and now automatically she laid what she would need beside the open suitcase on the bed. She wrapped shoes in tissue and put them in the bottom of the suitcase, then lingerie, and rolled several pairs of stockings and tucked them in the corners. Roberto hated women who were untidy and disorganized, who trailed through airports and railroad stations dragging packages and boxes. She took a black dress and folded tissue in the pleats of the skirt, two pairs of black gloves, a black lace mantilla that she wore when she attended Mass on Sundays. She had become a Catholic to please Roberto. Or was it to hold him so that he could never leave her?

Oh God, she thought, why did it have to be Peter? If You had to take one of my children, why couldn't it have been Marcia?

And then guilt flooded over her because she had never been able to love her daughter the way she should have. This plain large-boned girl who looked like Lathrop, who would rather buy a blanket for her horse than a ball gown, she was like a stranger, something she had borne that had no part of her.

But Peter. . . .

He was such a beautiful baby. Nurses would stop their prams in the park and exclaim over him. And he was an adorable little boy, she could still see him in his sailor suit feeding the bears at the zoo. He had always loved animals, he had a regular menagerie of pets. In fact, he seemed to prefer animals to people. Other children were jealous of him, that was why he wasn't invited to their homes often to play. And besides, she preferred to have him where Fräulein could supervise him and see that he didn't fall out of a tree or get roughed up by some bully. He had never broken a bone or had to have stitches in his face the way so many boys did.

Lathrop had thought it bad for him to grow up an only child, he wanted Peter to have brothers and sisters. She hadn't wanted any more children.

And then she found she was pregnant. She was furious. She had done everything to bring on a miscarriage. Nothing worked. The result was Marcia.

By then she had grown to hate Lathrop. And a year later she met Roberto.

It was July. She had taken Peter to Virginia Beach, leaving Marcia in the New York apartment with Lathrop and the nurse. They stayed at the Cavalier Hotel and a dark, handsome man who had the next beach cabana kept staring at her. She found out he was Roberto Carvalho, the Brazilian Ambassador. A red-haired woman was with him. She had asked if it was his wife. "No, he's not married," she was informed. "That's just a friend." This was accompanied by a wink and much laughter.

One morning she was strolling along a path in the hotel gardens, enjoying the beauty of the flowers and the sea air and the feeling of freedom. Peter had run on ahead chasing a butterfly. Suddenly Roberto Carvalho appeared with a camera and snapped her picture.

"Why did you do that?" she asked in an icy tone, thinking that she did not care to be added to this Latin lover's collection of lady friends, and at the same time wishing she had met him before she had met Lathrop.

"Because you have the most beautiful eyes I have ever seen," he said. "I could not resist. Forgive me." He nodded and walked on.

The next day he and his lady friend were gone.

Nina walked out on the balcony. Where is Roberto now that I need him? she thought bitterly. With another lady friend? A new conquest? All those Brazilian men had mistresses, it was the accepted thing, but it was something that she could never accept.

At least Lathrop hadn't wanted anyone else.

She gripped the balcony railing. Was she being punished? If she had not left Lathrop, would this terrible thing have happened? Had she neglected her children in the years when they were growing up and needed her?

Useless questions, too late. Who could turn back the past?

Voices drifted up from Avenida Atlantica. A truck filled with workers singing on their way home from work. She could see Corcovado in the distance, and on its peak the colossal statue of Christ with arms outstretched looming over the favelas, those shanty-towns in the hills where the poor lived. The sky had turned from mauve to gray. Any moment the lights round the bay would come on, sparkling in a long line from Botofoga to Ipanema.

Where are you now, Roberto?

She shivered. Never had she felt so alone, even in those awful days of her childhood in Baltimore. She was raised by an aunt and uncle after her parents were killed in an automobile accident. They lived in a red brick house with white steps in a row of houses one indistinguishable from the other, and she had to wear her cousin's hand-me-down clothes. How she envied the rich girls at school with their pretty dresses! When the other girls bought movie magazines at the corner drugstore she saved her allowance for *Vogue* and *Harper's Bazaar* and she studied how the society women in them dressed. She knew her only chance of escape was to make a wealthy marriage.

She had escaped. She never returned to Baltimore after her marriage to Lathrop.

When she passed through Baltimore in later years and saw the rows of flat-roofed houses from the train window it all seemed like a distant dream. But by then she was an ambassador's wife and one of the women pictured in the fashion magazines.

She had attained all she had wished for. And now, suddenly none of it mattered.

"Have you decided to leave me, *querida*? I know I have not been perhaps the best husband in the world, but. . . ."

She turned quickly. She was so absorbed in her thoughts that she had not heard Roberto come in. He was standing by the bed looking at the packed suitcase.

"Oh, Roberto!" She threw herself into his arms. "I'm so glad you're here. I thought you'd never come!"

"But you've been crying." He wiped a tear from her cheek. "What is the matter? I have never seen you cry before."

"It's Peter. Something awful has happened."

"Ah, my darling, it cannot be that bad. Remember the time—"

"He's been killed."

"No." Roberto looked stunned.

"He's dead. Murdered." She started to sob wildly. She knew that he had been expecting to be told of some scrape that Peter was involved in, like the time he was kicked out of prep school at Andover for sneaking a girl into his room. What did he care about her son, anyway?

"Did Ruth Ann call you?"

"Her name is Ruth Ellen. No, it was some awful Texas sheriff. He said I should come right away. They want to ask some questions."

"But can't his father answer anything they want to know?"

"But I am his mother." She looked at Roberto in amazement.

"Yes, of course. I know how dreadful this is for you, my darling, but what purpose would be served by you going to Texas?"

"The purpose is for my son's funeral."

"Yes, I understand, but there will be reporters from the newspapers and unpleasant questions. Under the circumstances, it seems to me that his father—"

"You never liked him anyway!" She started to beat the bed with her fists. "You drove him away from me, he was never welcome at the embassy, and don't think he didn't feel that!"

"Let us not go into these things now. You are distraught, the whole thing has been a terrible shock. I will call Doctor Silva to give you something to calm you."

"I don't like Doctor Silva. I want an American doctor."

"Doctor Silva has been the doctor to my family for many years. Let me handle this, my dearest. I know what is best."

And he started to speak rapidly into the phone in Portuguese.

Marcia had not cried since the news of her brother's death. She had never in her life been able to shed real tears because she was born without tear ducts. Before this it had not mattered. Nothing in her past had ever affected her enough. She was tough and proud of it. She took her horse over the highest jumps without any feeling of fear. She cared little about her looks and half the time didn't bother about make-up.

"You should at least try to hide some of those freckles," her mother used to say in despair. "Or stay out of the sun."

Her mother had a thing about the sun. She always carried a parasol at the beach or wore a large-brimmed hat. She was obsessed with her beauty. Thank God I'm not a glamour girl, Marcia thought. Her face and arms were covered with freckles and she had broad shoulders and heavy legs. Her naturally curly sandy hair was cut short and all she had to do to it in the mornings was run a comb through it. Now she lay on the bed in frontier pants and a wrinkled checked shirt and deep sobs wracked her big-boned body and she wished she could cry real tears like other women.

But she wasn't like other women. . . .

She knew some people suspected her of being a lesbian. Maybe that was why she had married the first man who had asked her, to prove that she was like other women after all. But she wasn't. She had never been interested in the silly feminine things that other girls were when she was growing up. Their inane chatter and giggling bored her. She had a mind like a man's and she would much rather have been a man. Dances were agony for her. She always tried to lead and stepped on her partner's toes. She felt far more comfortable in a stable than in a ballroom. Making her debut was torture, but she went through with it to please her mother. She hated her mother, and yet, strangely, she wanted her approval.

Her mother had always preferred Peter, and from the beginning Marcia accepted this without jealousy. Her brother was like a god to her, and she loved him more than anything in the whole world. As children, she used to cover up for Peter when he was in trouble, even taking the blame for things he had done. Once he stole some jacks and a rubber ball from Woolworth's when no one was looking. It was wrong, but it would never have occurred to her to tell on him.

She got up and started to pace the room, her large freckled hands thrust in her pants pockets.

Her lawyer had told her that if she left Nevada for more than a day it would nullify her residency for divorce, and she had been here almost five weeks now. She was tempted to go anyway.

If she went for a ride perhaps she would feel better. It would work off some of this restless feeling.

This ranch had been recommended by a friend from Long Island who had stayed here. They catered to wealthy women who sat around in the evenings drinking and playing bridge while they waited for their six weeks to be up, then the brief court appearance with their lawyers, the sealed records of Nevada, and home again to start a new life. The walls echoed with stories of "that louse." Quite often the husband had someone waiting, usually a much younger woman who "understood" him and would give him a new image, while the wife had only bitterness for company in the lonely nights ahead and the plaintive voices of her children asking, "Isn't Daddy going to sleep here anymore?"

Well, at least she had no children to make explanations to, Marcia thought. Her marriage had been brief, slightly over a year. Long enough for her to discover that the titled Hungarian she thought loved her had only married her for the money he thought she would inherit from her father, and that his title was as phony as he was. She was asking the court to restore her maiden name and she hoped she would never have to see him again.

Over and done with. Almost. No, she could not leave. She could not cancel out all these weeks of waiting. Peter would understand. Peter had always understood.

She remembered how he used to escort her to dances when she didn't have a date. He was more fun to be with than any of the boys she knew, anyway. They used to laugh together about a lot of things that only they understood. He always shared everything with her.

Until Valerie. . . .

But that was after the war. He was different when he returned from overseas. He drifted for a while, he didn't want to go back to Princeton, he didn't seem to know what he wanted to do. It was during that period that he met Valerie.

Valerie seemed to affect him in a way that no other girl had before. She hated her, but she tried not to show it. She thought for a while that Peter was going to marry Valerie. Then quite suddenly he announced that he was going to try his luck in the oil business. He left, and she never saw him again.

Now, she never would.

She still couldn't understand how it happened. What was it he had said once when they were children together? She tried to remember. There was a poem of Rupert Brooke's he used to quote . . . something about the rain and death. Had he always had a premonition of tragedy, that he would die young?

Her father said he was going to get his own private investigator, he was going to personally track down Peter's killer and bring him to justice. "Those trigger-happy Texans," he said on the phone. "They have a murder a day there. What does one more matter to them?" His voice broke. "My son, he was my only son. . . ."

And I'm your only daughter, Father, remember? I have feelings too, but I'm not supposed to break down. Good old reliable Marcia. The brick, you used to call me. Things don't affect me. It was Peter everyone worried about. Was it because he was sickly when he was little and I wasn't? Was that why he got all the attention? Or was it because he was handsome and I wasn't? I don't really mind not being pretty, but I just want someone to notice that I have feelings like everyone else.

"Call me when you get to Texas, Father."

Will Mother be there, I wonder? And Uncle Roberto? Better not to ask. Old wounds, reopened. "That nigger Brazilian," her father had once called him. "They all have a touch of the tarbrush in Brazil. Even in the best families."

She had never liked her stepfather, but he certainly didn't look as if he had Negro blood.

"You know the first question a Brazilian father asks the doctor when his child is born? Not 'Is it a boy?' but 'Is it white?'" Her father had laughed uproariously at this joke.

Spare me from ever having children who are caught in the middle between two parents whose love has turned to hate. I'm glad Miklos and I didn't have a child. I never want children.

Never. . . .

She ran her fingers through her cropped hair and, clenching her teeth, she flung open the door and strode rapidly in the direction of the stables.

"Ladies and gentlemen, we will be arriving in Dallas in a few minutes. Please see that your seat belts are fastened and observe the NO SMOKING sign. Thank you."

Lathrop glanced out the plane window. Dallas lay under a bank of clouds. He would have over an hour's wait here before changing to a smaller plane for Midland. He put out his cigarette. They were slowly descending, but he could see nothing.

"Instrument landing," said the man across the aisle.

Lathrop merely nodded, not wanting to get into a conversation.

The man tried again. "Amazing the way pilots handle these big planes."

Peter had wanted to be a pilot, Lathrop recalled. It was during the early part of the war. He quit Princeton and tried to enlist in the Air Corps. It looked as if they were going to take him until it was discovered that as a boy he had asthma. He tried to convince the doctors on the medical board that he no longer had attacks. It was no use. Lathrop remembered how disappointed Peter was. That was the end of his dream of being a flier.

Instead he wound up in the Army Signal Corps. He went through Officers' Candidate School at Fort Monmouth, New Jersey and emerged a second lieutenant with crossed flags on his lapel instead of wings. Shortly after that he was sent overseas.

In the following months when Lathrop read the newspapers and listened to the war reports on the radio he was glad that Peter was not in the Air Force. Too many of our planes were being shot down. At least the Signal Corps was fairly safe.

Had they always tried to protect Peter too much? The doctor had told him one time that Peter's asthmatic attacks were emotional. That was after they had given him all kinds of allergy tests, removed his pillow, eliminated certain foods, and still could not find the cause.

But the attacks were pretty frightening. Never would he forget the sight of Peter's pale face on the pillow gasping for breath, the awful wheezing and whistling sounds as he fought to get air in his lungs. Steam, more steam. Oil of eucalyptus.

"Doctor, can't you do something?"

"It will pass."

The nights he sat by Peter's bed watching helplessly. Sometimes it seemed that he would expire at any minute. But the attacks always passed, and as Peter grew older they stopped entirely.

He felt the wheels touch the runway and the plane taxied to a stop. They had landed.

He followed the other passengers down the aisle. The stewardess was saying goodbye to everyone. Someone commented on the heavy drizzle outside.

"A little Texas mist," she laughed.

Relatives and friends greeted the arriving passengers. "How y'all? Have a good trip?" He pushed his way through the crowd. No one was meeting him here and he had to check on his flight to Midland.

"Lathrop Spaulding?" A young man in a raincoat came up to him.

"Yes."

"Associated Press." He flashed a press card. "Could we have a statement from you please?"

"I'm sorry . . . I have nothing to say." He brushed the young man aside and walked quickly into the building. Reporters, damn them, he thought. It was just starting. Wanting all the gory details, the reactions of the bereaved. "The victim's father is holding up as well as can be expected." He passed the newsstand. WASHINGTON SOCIALITE SLAIN IN MIDLAND, read one headline. STEPSON OF FORMER BRAZILIAN AMBASSADOR MURDERED. MYSTERIOUS FOE KILLS PETER SPAULDING. The papers were full of it.

Two elderly women passed.

"Minnie Lee, what do those there headlines say? I don't have my glasses."

"Oh, just another of them murders."

"Well, let's buy a paper anyway. I want to read all about it."

He walked on. Stepson of former Brazilian Ambassador. Anything to sell newspapers. That bastard Carvalho. That's when it all started. He felt his throat constrict and drops of sweat broke out on his forehead. He was trembling all over. Not here. He must control himself. He clenched his fists.

"Can I help you?"

It was a priest in a long black robe. Damned bead rattlers. What was one doing here? He looked out of place in Texas.

"No . . . thank you."

Those damn Catholics. What was it they said? "Give me a child until he's four. . . ." Nina had become a Catholic when she married Carvalho. She had gotten an annulment of her marriage to him so that she and Carvalho could be married by a priest.

"Doesn't that make our children bastards?" he asked.

"Of course not!" She had glared at him coldly. He could smell again the scent of "Bellodgia" that she always wore.

"Then how did you get an annulment? I thought you had to prove fraud. Or did you tell the priest that our marriage was never consummated?"

"You needn't be sarcastic. I think you know on what grounds I obtained it."

Yes, he knew. He hated her. He hated her for her lack of compassion. Her selfishness. Her beauty. There is no love so intense as that which has turned to hate. Like an unquenchable fire, its flame burned on the altars of his soul day and night. Forgive. An easy word. Bless those who have hurt you. Lines, spoken by idiots. He wanted her to suffer. To suffer as much as she had made him suffer.

He remembered something his mother had said to him after she met Nina.

"She'll hurt you, son. She has nothing, she comes from a very modest background, and she wants everything. She'll leave you the minute someone else comes along."

His mother lived long enough to see her unhappy prophecy come true.

"May I see your ticket, sir?"

He handed his ticket to the airline clerk, who stamped it and handed it back.

"Your plane for Midland leaves from Gate 7, sir. You may board in forty-five minutes."

"Thank you."

Forty-five minutes until his flight for Hell. Who said there was no such place?

NINE

*T*unnels. Tunnels that are dark and winding and have no end. The tunnels around Baltimore. Where is the light? There is no light. Only the eternal darkness and Peter dead, Peter dead in the dark, Peter crying for help. Now he is a little boy again. Mummy, I'm afraid of the dark, I hate the tunnels. We'll pull down the shades, see, now you can't see the tunnels. But I can feel them, I'm afraid. Look, your sister isn't afraid, and she's a girl. Boys have to be brave. Is Daddy brave? Of course, all men are brave. Now, we've passed the tunnels, we'll pull up the shades. We've passed Baltimore. Do we have to go under the river, Mummy, before we get to New York? I don't like that either. I hate the dark.

The world is all dark. Black, like the tunnels. And Peter is dead. My son is dead.

Turn back the years. Begin again. Everything will be so different. It is the night he is born. I have a son. I am so happy. He is perfect, there is nothing wrong with him. I was so afraid there might be. But no, he is beautiful. His life is all ahead of him. What will he be, my son?

Nina, don't leave me. Think of our children. I'll do anything you want, but don't leave me.

I love Roberto. I've never loved you, Lathrop. Not really.

You'll pay for this, Nina. You'll suffer.

It is Christmas Eve. I am seven years old. I am waiting for my father and mother under the Christmas tree. There are presents that I have wrapped for them. I made them at school. The tree has strings of popcorn and candy canes and paper ornaments and lights. Outside it is snowing. The streets shine with ice. So pretty. The Christmas tree and the snow. And then a policeman at the door. Mandy, what has happened? Pore chile, pore chile. Christmas is over.

The train goes by and shakes the house. I hate this house with its flat roof and the soot from the train. Someday I will get on one of those trains and never come back. I will have a pretty house and clothes. Not these ugly dresses. I will never mend a torn dress, I will throw it away. Nothing will hurt me again. No one will make me cry. Ever.

The tunnel has no light. I cannot breathe. The train is a long black snake. Turn on the lights. There is a roaring and thunder.

Ma'am, there's been an accident.

Wake up, Nina, wake up. It was a dream. It is morning and the street sounds of Rio are starting, another day, another day. It was not a dream. It all happened. It really happened. Carnations. White carnations in a jade bowl beside the bed. Like a funeral. Take them away! But they're your favorite flowers. You always have vases of white carnations. Like the perfume you wear, "Bellodgia." I hate it!

A voice in the next room. Roberto. He is talking on the telephone. What is he saying?

The carnations are on the floor. There is water on the bed and broken pieces of jade. Maria! Clean it up. The doorbell is ringing. Why don't you answer it? Where is everyone?

The phone again. I will listen on the extension. How quickly Roberto picks it up. He does not want me to answer.

"I'm sorry, but my wife cannot come to the telephone. I am sure you will understand. She is completely desolated by this terrible tragedy. The doctor has placed her under heavy sedation. . . . No, I do not think she will be able to attend the funeral. Yes . . . Yes, it has all been such a shock. He was like my own son. A fine boy."

Liar! You never cared about him!

I will get dressed. Where have you put my suitcase? I *will* go! You can't stop me. Peter . . . Peter. Oh, my God. It's not true, it's not true. You're not dead.

"Nina . . . *querida,* go back to bed. You must rest. I have taken care of everything. Here, let me help you."

"No. I'm getting up. Where did you put my suitcase?"

"My dearest, you are in no condition to take a trip. Be careful, you will cut yourself on the jade. That beautiful bowl. What a shame! It has been in my family for generations."

What is that compared to the loss of my son? I'm glad it's broken! It can never be mended. Nothing can ever be mended. Everything is smashed like the jade bowl.

"Maria, please clean this up and bring Senhora Carvalho some breakfast."

"I'm not hungry."

"You must keep up your strength. It is necessary for you to eat something"

"All right." She leaned back wearily. "I'll try."

"Good." He dismissed Maria and sat on the edge of the bed caressing Nina's hand as he spoke. "*Querida,* the newspapers and wire services are calling constantly. I think it best if we go away for a few days where they do not know where to reach us. We can open up the house at Petropólis. You have always liked it there. No one will think to look for us there in the off-season."

Petropólis. High in the mountains. Hydrangeas everywhere, in the gardens and parks and lining the streets. She thought of Curupião, her pet oriole, sitting on a blue hydrangea bush singing, his brilliant yellow body and black wings contrasting with the flowers. Picking bits of mamaõ from between her fingers at breakfast, his black beady eyes watching her. The scent of mimosa. A huge lizard sunning himself. Tiny pink orchids growing wild in the trees. Bougainvillea and bamboo. Petrópolis! How unreal it all seemed now!

"From what are we running, Roberto?"

"I am only thinking of you, my dearest."

Are you? she thought. Or of the Carvalho name involved in unsavory headlines? She pushed him away.

"I am going to my son's funeral, Roberto. I am going whether you want me to or not. There is no way you can stop me." She stood up, clutching the carved jacarandá bedpost for support. "Now, please have Maria bring me my suitcase."

Ruth Ellen stood staring at Peter's clothes hanging in the closet. All that was left. This was the bitter reality, the mute testimony. The utter emptiness. His ties, neatly on a rack. The striped one he had been wearing the day she met him. The tweed jacket she loved. Waiting. Waiting for him to put it on. His shoes, polished and in shoe trees. Everything in order, on the surface. They had gone through the pockets, the trousers, looking for messages, names, numbers, a slip of paper that might reveal a clue, anything. There was nothing.

She wandered aimlessly over to the bureau and opened a drawer. The blue alpaca sweater that she had given him last Christmas, their one and only Christmas together....

How happy she was then! She had just found out she was pregnant. They trimmed a small tree together and she thought, at this time next year there will be three of us. Peter told her that he hated Christmas. It brought back something painful from his childhood. He would not tell her what it was. Never mind, she would make it all up to him. The baby would change all that. Peter would be a wonderful father. She could picture the expression on his face playing with his son, tucking him in at night. The fun they would have. How lucky she was! How good life could be.

Gone. All of it gone.

No, there was still the baby. She was being selfish and thinking only of herself.

She opened another drawer. Peter's socks, his handkerchiefs, a box of cufflinks. She picked up the box and then she saw something silver in the corner of the drawer. A key. It must have been there all the time and Ruth Ellen wondered why she had not noticed it before. She turned it in her fingers, trying to think what it would fit.

It didn't look like a key for a trunk or a suitcase, it was more the kind of key—yes, that was it—it was for a padlock.

Where had she seen a padlock?

And then she remembered. The garage. Peter kept an old army locker in the back of the garage. Once she had asked him why he didn't get rid of it and he had given her a funny look and said there were things in it he wanted to keep.

What things? she wondered.

She clutched the key and went out to the garage.

The locker was buried under a pile of empty cardboard boxes and fertilizer sacks. She tried to lift it but it was too heavy. She knelt down on the concrete floor and put the key in the padlock. It was rusty and hard to turn but finally she got it open.

There was Peter's army uniform and his medals and some snapshots taken during the war with men she had never seen who had shared his life. There was a revolver, but not the kind her father had carried, it looked foreign and she wondered if it were German. She looked at it more closely. Yes, it must be a German Luger. She put it down carefully. There was a book of fairy tales written in German with lovely old-fashioned pictures. A postcard of a quaint old town, Freudenstadt. A small book of poems by Rupert Brooke. And a yellowed newspaper clipping.

She unfolded it. It was a picture of a girl, a girl with fine chiseled features and long fair hair, wearing a ball gown. "Miss Valerie Blair, daughter of Senator Everitt Blair, one of this season's leading debutantes."

Now she knew. Valerie Blair. She was the one who had lain between them at night, whose name he whispered in his sleep, the one who caused the far-off look in Peter's eyes, the one he had really wanted. No, it wasn't true, Peter had married her. Didn't that prove something? What did an old love in a faded newspaper picture mean? She wasn't real.

But why had Peter kept the picture, even after he had married her? Why was he so indifferent, never speaking of love, treating her almost like a sister? She was always the one who had initiated their infrequent love-making, not he.

She felt sick. If only she had not opened the locker.

Had Valerie come back into Peter's life? Was it she who made those phone calls and then hung up? This was the worst kind of torture. Now she would never know.

Valerie Blair, Valerie Blair, she kept repeating to herself. What had she meant in Peter's life?

She looked at the clipping again and then she crumpled it up. This was something that Sheriff Mahoney would never see. Or anyone else.

TEN

*V*alerie Blair stood in front of the Lakeside Summer Playhouse where she was the ingenue in the resident company and looked at her name on the poster.

The play was *The Glass Menagerie* and this week's guest star was the aging Hollywood film actress, Gladys Walker, who was making her comeback via summer stock after being "in retirement" for a number of years, the retirement having been spent mostly in an alcoholic sanitarium. Gladys Walker had the role of a faded Southern belle and Valerie was playing her crippled daughter.

"This child is much too pretty to play Laura," Gladys Walker announced the first day of rehearsal. "Laura is meant to be shy, plain, introverted. It won't be convincing. Get someone else." She pulled at her sagging jowls and gave the stage manager instructions to use only pink lights.

"Please give her a chance, Miss Walker," the director said. "After all, the audience has come to see you. When you are on stage, who will look at anyone else?"

"Well, I suppose you're right. If she can look washed out with stringy hair. . . ." She looked dubiously at Valerie's long golden hair and deep violet eyes. "It's nothing against you, my dear, it's the way Tennessee Williams wrote it."

"I can assure you that she will be convincing as Laura," the director said. "Now, shall we get on with the rehearsal? We only have five days." He walked over and picked up his script. "Let's hope our star stays off the booze," he whispered to the stage manager.

The dress rehearsal was a disaster. Gladys Walker kept forgetting her lines and complaining about the huge New Jersey mosquitoes and the firecrackers exploding around the lake.

"But it *is* the Fourth of July. Let's be thankful we open tomorrow night, not tonight." Matt Bernstein had found from past experience that it didn't pay to let the star get the upper hand. The director must hold the reins at all times and he intended to do so. "Temperamental bitch," he mumbled to himself. He called to one of the apprentices to spray Miss Walker's dressing room with Flit. "And check that pot of tea she's drinking," he said.

The next morning there was a line rehearsal and Gladys Walker managed to trip over one of the props and went sprawling across the stage. At first they thought she had broken her arm. A doctor was hastily summoned and it turned out to be a chipped bone in the elbow. He taped it and suggested the show be postponed. This roused Gladys Walker from her alcoholic stupor.

"But all these poor people have come to see me!" she wailed. "We can't just refund their money and turn them away. It's out of the question. I'll go on anyway." She drew herself up. "It's my return to the theatre after sixteen years. I won't disappoint my public. We'll open as scheduled."

Valerie noticed that she slurred "scheduled." Or else she was pronouncing it in British fashion. Poor old thing, Valerie thought. She had seen Gladys Walker in movies when she was a little girl and admired her talent. Though never a real beauty, Gladys Walker had a certain quality that came across. It was hard to find it now. She was short and dumpy and her heavy makeup did little to conceal the crow's feet and puffy, blotched complexion.

Could I become like that one day? Valerie wondered. It was a terrifying idea. At twenty, middle age seemed far away. And everything was going so beautifully now. This part that she'd been dying to do ever since she had seen Julie Hayden play it on Broadway. And her agent said she was all set for the ingenue in the new John van Druten play starting rehearsals the end of August. It would be her first Broadway show. Soon she would be recognized on her own, she wouldn't just be known as Senator Blair's daughter. Even Daddy thought I'd quit after a few weeks of making rounds, she thought. Everyone thought I'd come running back to Washington and go to a lot of silly teas and do Junior League work. Well, I'll surprise them all! I'm going to be someone in the theatre.

"Suppose you do become a star?" Peter Spaulding had asked her one night sitting at the Stork Club. "What would you have that you don't have now?"

Strange, she had been thinking about Peter a lot the past week. He had never understood her wanting to act. It had been two years now since she'd seen him. Someone told her that he'd gotten married to a Texas girl. The news upset her far more than she expected. When he went to Midland she thought, I'll put time and space between us. I'll forget him. But deep down she assured herself, He'll be back.

She heard the director's voice. "All right, cast. Be at the theatre tonight at seven-thirty."

The opening was a huge success. Gladys Walker, in true trouper fashion, pulled herself together and gave a great performance. The long flowing sleeves of her costume hid her taped elbow, and if she was in pain, no one knew it. They had curtain call after curtain call. She does still have a public, Valerie thought. The elderly ladies staying at the Lake Hopatcong Inn gushed backstage, waving programs to be autographed.

Even Matt Bernstein looked relaxed and happy, for a change. "Great job, Valerie," he said.

"You were excellent, my dear," Gladys Walker said. "I told Mr. Bernstein you'd be just right in the part."

However when the reviews came out the next day, Gladys Walker was less gracious. Her own notices were good, but a lot of space was given to Valerie's performance.

"Playing the crippled daughter was a young actress of extraordinary talent and beauty, Valerie Blair," said one newspaper critic. "A sensitive, fragile quality that was deeply moving," read another review.

From then on there was a distinct chill in the air. The star did not care to have attention drawn to anyone else. She made things as difficult as possible for Valerie, inventing bits of business to do on Valerie's lines and upstaging her at every possible opportunity.

Oh well, it's only until the end of the week, Valerie thought. She was busy rehearsing in the daytime for her role in next week's production of *My Sister Eileen*. Eileen was another of those pretty, empty-headed heroines that it was hard to do anything with. She liked parts that she could really get her teeth into. But it was all good experience, she told herself.

She walked along the lake back to the inn, her script tucked under her arm. She had about two hours to study her lines for *Eileen*, then a quick shower and dinner and back to the theatre to play Laura. This summer stock was really exhausting, but she loved it.

Why do you have to prove something to yourself? a voice whispered. We could have been happy.

She and Peter were really so alike, yet neither had been willing to give in and see the other's point of view. She had tried to persuade him to get a job in New York instead. He had refused. Should she have given up everything and gone with him the way pioneer women followed their men out West? The thought of living in a place like Midland was like death to her. Or worse than death.

"If you really loved me, you'd marry me and come with me," he had told her on that rainy April afternoon in Washington.

"But I do love you."

"No. Not enough."

"Peter . . . try to understand."

"Oh, I understand all right."

"No, you don't."

"Just once in my life I'd like to have someone love me without reservations. To be with me all the way. I've never had that."

"Peter . . . this is something I have to do. I have to . . . well, prove that I can do something on my own. To prove that I'm any good, I guess."

"It doesn't make sense. You're beautiful, you have everything that a lot of other girls would like to have. And I love you. Doesn't that mean anything to you?"

"Yes, but. . . ."

"What's the use? Goodbye, Valerie."

"Peter, I *do* love you."

"In your way. It's not enough."

And he had left. He wrote several times from Midland, and then the letters stopped. He did not come back.

Not enough. Not enough. The words echoed in her head.

The dirt road along the lake had been oiled to keep down the dust. Goldenrod and daisies grew in clumps beside the road and she stopped and picked a daisy. Children were swimming in the lake and a sailboat skimmed across the water. If only I had time for a swim, she thought. Usually she had a deep tan in the summer, but what little she had gotten before leaving Washington had faded.

She remembered summers spent at Rehoboth Beach when her mother was alive, with her older sister Adele, and her father arriving on weekends with a briefcase of work and bills he had to study.

"You might as well stay in Washington, Everitt," her mother used to say. "You never relax."

"Jessica, my love, I'm afraid that's what you get for marrying a politician."

Her father was twenty years older than her mother and busy campaigning when they met. It was a whirlwind courtship. He proposed on their second date and they were married six weeks later.

"I didn't want to give your mother a chance to say no," her father said. "She had too many other beaux hanging around."

The Washington climate never agreed with her mother's delicate constitution, and every winter she had sieges of bronchitis. One bitter cold March the bronchitis turned into pneumonia. They waited for the crisis to pass. It was an awful night. Her mother was in an oxygen tent. Finally her father came downstairs where she was waiting with Adele. Tears were streaming down his cheeks and he was shaking with sobs. She had never seen her father cry before and it frightened her.

"Damn those doctors!" he said. "Why couldn't they save her? Why?"

It took her a long time to realize that she would never see her mother again. Her father buried himself even more in his work. At eighteen Adele eloped with a Belgian count. They moved to Brussels, and when the war came their château was occupied by the Germans. Adele now had two children and her life with the count was less than idyllic.

"Don't marry as young as I did," she warned Valerie on one of her visits to Washington. "Have all the fun you can first."

She had been very lonely after Adele married and moved to Europe. In spite of the fact that Adele was seven years older, they had always been very close. Her father was overly strict and he did not know how to show affection. She could understand why Adele had wanted to get away.

Their house on Massachusetts Avenue filled with antiques and Oriental rugs depressed her too. Nothing had been changed since her mother's death.

She had sensed the same loneliness in Peter when they first met. His life had not been too unlike hers. She had never met his father, but she knew Senhora Carvalho and thought her beautiful, but cold. She could never imagine her changing diapers or taking care of a sick child. Peter had told her one time that he hated her. She had been shocked.

"But she's your mother," she had protested, thinking of her own mother and wishing she were still alive.

"So that means I'm supposed to love her? Because she's my mother? Well I don't. She doesn't give a darn what happens to me or to Marcia. All she cares about is going to parties and whether some fag dress designer puts her on his best-dressed list."

He told her about the episode at Andover. Someone had dared him to bring a waitress from the local tavern back to the dorm and he had been caught and kicked out. She suspected that he really wanted to be expelled to get his mother's attention. She was on a Mediterranean cruise at the time. She wrote him a letter saying: "Peter darling, really, how could you do anything so stupid?" But she had not interrupted her cruise.

His father had laughed about it and called him a "chip off the old block."

"Do you think your father would like me?" she once asked Peter.

"I'm sure he would. He likes all pretty girls."

"That's not exactly a compliment."

"I didn't mean it that way. Yes, my father would like you."

But he seemed in no hurry to introduce her to his father and when finally they did meet it was only for a brief cocktail in the Oak Room of the Plaza Hotel.

She continued along the road. Last night the strangest thing had happened. It was about midnight and she was in her room studying her script after the performance. Suddenly she looked up and saw Peter standing in her room. She thought she must be dreaming. He looked just the way he had on that rainy afternoon in Washington two years ago.

She stared at him, unable to speak.

"I wanted to see you once more. I've never forgotten you, Valerie."

His face had the saddest expression she had ever seen.

"I'll always love you. Remember that."

"Peter. . . ." You've come back, she thought. I always knew you would. She reached out her arms to him, but there was nothing there, only shadows. "Peter?"

No answer. Had she been dreaming? No, it was all too clear for a dream. He had been there. Peter had come back to her, and then just as suddenly, he had vanished again.

What did it all mean?

ELEVEN

*I*t was almost time to leave for the airport. Nina walked out on the balcony and looked down at the city. How much had happened since yesterday when she last looked at this view that she had always loved, the ever-changing bay of Rio, its blue mountain peaks with wisps of clouds against a pink sky, ships in the harbor unloading passengers and cargo, the scurrying crowds along the black-and-white mosaic sidewalks, honking of horns, life going on as usual.

When she was a little girl in Baltimore she once prayed: "Whatever my life is, don't let it be dull. I can bear anything but that."

The fingers that have shaped us. When we are small we are like soft clay, easily molded; later we are like granite, a chisel is needed to change the shape of what we have become. And so it was with Nina.

During the delirium of the night she remembered a priest standing by her bed. A thin, serious priest with glasses and a high, nasal voice mumbling in Latin. It was Roberto's brother, Otavio. He had been promised to the church by their mother when he was a little boy, as a reward for his recovery from a grave illness. Otavio was the second son. The eldest, João, was a prosperous businessman in São Paulo. Roberto was the youngest and his mother's favorite.

Elizinha Carvalho had never forgiven her favorite son for

marrying a fallen woman: a divorcee. She was the daughter of a wealthy sugar plantation owner from Recife, a devout Catholic who went to Mass every day to pray for the soul of her long departed husband. She still dressed all in black and never went out without a long crepe veil and black gloves. Frequently she dabbed at her eyes with a black-bordered handkerchief. With Otavio she visited the favelas and took baskets of food and clothing to the poor. Her bedroom was filled with religious statues and pictures of the Redeemer. Happiness was not for this life but the next, for those who obeyed His will. This life was to be endured for the greater reward. Her martyred and melancholy air pervaded everything.

Elizinha Carvalho had sent a message with Otavio. "My mother wishes me to convey to you her deepest condolences," he said. One eyelid twitched behind his thick glasses and he fumbled with his rosary. "My mother said to tell you that she will have a Mass said at Nossa Senhora da Gloria de Oteiro."

"Thank you." She did not know what else to say. She had never understood the Catholic fetish of having masses said for the dead so that their souls would not remain in limbo in Purgatory. It was one of the several things about the Catholic religion that no priest had been able to satisfactorily explain to her, but she knew that having a special Mass said was very important to a Catholic. "That is very kind of your mother, Otavio."

Otavio bowed stiffly, said a few prayers and left. Nina was glad his mother had not come. She always looked at her daughter-in-law as if she felt she deserved the fires of Hell. Nina wondered if Elizinha Carvalho had ever really known love. Her marriage to Roberto's father had been arranged by their families. She had done her duty and borne him three sons before he passed on to an early grave, but had she ever been in love with him, really in love? Nina doubted it, in spite of her daily trips to the altar to pray for him. How harsh in their judgments of others are those who have never been tempted, how easy to say righteously, "I would never do that," until one day the occasion arises and you are faced with the choice.

She thought of her other mother-in-law, Gertrude Spaulding, who died during the war. She, too, had made harsh judgments. Nina had never felt comfortable with her but both Peter and Marcia were devoted to her, and she spoiled them to death whenever they visited Wynwood. Well, no wonder, she thought bitterly. Roberto had never wanted children around, and she must have known that. But he had no right to try to turn them against her.

Do most women resent the girl their only son marries, as if losing him to a rival? She thought guiltily of Ruth Ellen and how she had condemned her without even having met her. No doubt she was very sweet, but she didn't sound like the kind of girl who would interest Peter. But then, no girl ever lasted long with Peter and she was glad, she hadn't wanted him to get serious and marry before going off to war the way so many of his friends did. War put crazy pressures on young people, it made them do things they wouldn't normally do. She was glad Peter had been sensible.

What good was being sensible when danger lurked everywhere, behind every unopened door, like a game of Russian roulette. Who could know when the empty chamber suddenly had a bullet? And then it was all over.

Peter's life was over.

No, it was not true. She simply could not believe it. She would not believe it until she saw his body, and she knew she could not face that. To see her baby, her beautiful child, white and stiff with bullet holes in him, it was more than she could bear.

The things that happened were beyond human endurance.

She had been angry with Roberto. Maybe this was what he had hoped to spare her. He knew it would be too much for her. But no one can spare us in life, she thought. She had to face it somehow.

"Are you ready, my darling?" Roberto came into the bedroom, a look of concern on his face.

"Yes." She closed her suitcase and locked it.

They heard laughter and shrieks from the kitchen.

"It is Maria," Roberto said. "She has won the *jogo do bicho*."

All the Brazilian servants played the daily lottery, spent their hard-earned money on the slim chance of being a winner, even when their families had scarcely enough to eat.

"I'll tell her to be quiet," Roberto said.

Nina put a restraining hand on his arm. "No," she said. "It's all right."

"Do you have everything?" Roberto asked.

"Yes." She took a final glance around the room and then pulled the black veil over her face.

In the courthouse at Midland, Sheriff Mahoney sifted the pile of papers on his desk and shook his head.

"It's like trying to look for a needle in a haystack," he said to the Texas Ranger sitting across from him. "I reckon we've checked on every deal Spaulding's made since he's been in Texas and talked to everyone here who knew him."

"No clues?"

"Only that one man did the killing. We found footprints in the mud beside the house and had casts made of them. And we got the bullets, two from the body and one in a tree trunk. They were shot from a .38."

"Not much to go on. You don't know of anyone who had a grudge against him?"

"He hadn't an enemy that we can find. Everyone liked him."

"This earlier attempt on his life—how long ago was that?"

"March of last year."

"Sixteen months ago?"

"Yeah." The sheriff spat into a brass spittoon.

"What happened then?"

"Young Spaulding had an apartment with another oil company employee, David Creighton—"

"This was before he was married then?"

"Yeah, he didn't even know his wife then according to our records, and she seemed surprised when we told her about the shooting. Guess he didn't want her to know about it."

"Or wasn't worried about it. You say he didn't even have a gun on him when he was found?"

"No, but he was worried, all right. He came to us right after Creighton was shot and asked us to protect him."

"Why did they shoot Creighton if they were after Spaulding?"

"A mistake. At least that's what Creighton told us. He lost an eye. Someone shot through the window of the apartment but Spaulding wasn't there. He had just left."

"I see. Where is Creighton now? I'd like to talk to him."

"He's moved to Colorado. He got out of the oil business after that."

"Can't say as I blame him. Was the bullet that hit Creighton from the same gun as the ones you got from Spaulding's body?"

"It was a .38 in both cases. Whether it was from the same revolver, well, your guess is as good as mine." Sheriff Mahoney spat into the spittoon again.

The Ranger studied the report. "I see there were other attempts to kill Spaulding after that."

"Sure were. Whoever did it wasn't playing games."

"Tools dropped on him in the oil fields, his car was tampered with and he narrowly missed death on a curve driving home, his house was set afire another time. . . ."

"Someone sure wanted him out of the way."

"And all this time your office was protecting him?"

"What were we supposed to do? Assign a full-time bodyguard to him? We don't have enough men for that." He didn't like the question or the sarcasm in the Ranger's voice. Let the Texas Rangers see if they had any better luck tracking down the killer.

"When is Spaulding's father arriving?"

"Any time now."

"Good. There are several questions I want to ask him."

Lathrop had dozed off, and now he opened his eyes and saw that the plane was losing altitude. He pulled back the curtain and saw below a vast wasteland, barren and desolate, and in the distance what appeared to be a cluster of skyscrapers emerging from a brown mist. This must be Midland, he thought, and again he cursed Fate, who had lured his only son to this bleak place to die.

The doorbell rang, the chime sound that Peter had installed himself because he said it reminded him of the grandfather clock they had at Wynwood, and then it was drowned out by Tornado's barking.

"Hush," Ruth Ellen said. She looked out the living room window and saw a taxi pulling away from the curb. He's here, she thought, Peter's father, and she opened the front door and saw a tall, heavy-set man with sandy-gray hair who was carrying a suitcase.

"Ruth Ellen?" His voice sounded so much like Peter's that it gave her a shock, even though he looked nothing like him. She couldn't see his eyes because he was wearing dark glasses.

"I'm so glad you're here," she said, wondering if she should call him "Mr. Spaulding" or "Dad," and then she threw herself into his arms and started to cry.

He patted her awkwardly and handed her his handkerchief.

"I'm sorry." She blew her nose. "I didn't think I could cry anymore."

He took off his dark glasses and she saw that his eyes were swollen and red-rimmed.

"I came straight from the airport," he said, indicating his suitcase. "I'll check in at the hotel later."

The telephone rang.

"Excuse me," she said. "Please sit down." She noticed him glance around the living room, taking in the furnishings. "Hello?... Yes ... Yes, he's here. He just arrived." She cupped her hand over the phone. "It's Sheriff Mahoney." She nodded. "Yes ... All right, I'll tell him."

Peter's father was stroking Tornado, who had stopped growling and was sitting at his feet.

"When Peter was small we had two beagles," he said. "We had this place in Maryland." He paused, remembering. "That was the sheriff, you say?"

"He's on his way over here."

The phone rang again and Ruth Ellen picked it up. "Hello? ... Yes, I'm fine. Peter's father just arrived and we're sitting here talking.... Thank you for bringing over the casserole. It was so sweet of you ... I know, I will eat something. I promise.... Yes, I'll call you if I need anything ... Goodbye."

"Our neighbors have been so kind," she said. "I don't know how I could have managed without them. The couple who live next door... that was she who just called... have been here most of the time. She had to go home to fix supper for her children. By the way, are you hungry?"

"No. But I could use a drink."

Ruth Ellen started to get up.

"I'll get it. Just tell me where it is."

"Over there. And there's ice in the kitchen through that door." She rubbed her back. It was starting to ache again. She felt so heavy and clumsy. Her hair was hanging like damp string around her pale face, devoid of all makeup since ... how long had it been now? She had lost all sense of time.

"Can I fix a drink for you, Ruth Ellen?"

"Maybe a light bourbon and water."

She leaned back wearily and closed her eyes, and her mind wandered back again. . . .

❖

After the barbecue at the Gilmore Ranch, Peter started calling her for dates two or three evenings a week. He never made plans in advance, it was always for that evening, and she made sure that she was there for his phone calls. Sometimes she wondered if she should pretend to be busy occasionally so he would think she was more popular and not just sitting by the phone waiting for him, but she had never been able to play games with men the way some girls did.

Some evenings they went to a movie, and other times they had dinner at the Scharbauer Hotel or just took a drive. Peter had a convertible and he liked to keep the top down. She told him about spring in Texas when the fields were covered with bluebonnets. She tried to make him see the Texas she loved with its vast plains and open skies that had more stars at night than any place else on earth.

"How do you know if you've never been out of Texas?" he kidded her.

"I just know, that's all."

One evening in the lobby of the Scharbauer Hotel a tall, sexy-looking redhead came up to Peter.

"Hi ya, honey."

Ruth Ellen noticed that her bright purple dress clung to her voluptuous figure and was cut low in front. Her sling pumps were studded with rhinestones and she carried a large glittering purse. Peter looked uncomfortable as he introduced them.

"Hello, Billie. This is Ruth Ellen Tyler . . . Billie Johnson."

"Pleased to meet you, I'm sure." Billie's eyes swept her from head to foot and then dismissed her. "Nice running into you," she said to Peter.

"Yes, it's good to see you, Billie. How's everything?"

"Everything's just fine, honey. See ya. Bye now."

"Goodbye, Billie."

Several men turned and winked knowingly as the flash of purple and flaming red swept through the door. Ruth Ellen caught a glimpse of a black Cadillac with steer horns on the front waiting at the hotel entrance. The occupant was honking impatiently. Billie quickly got in and the car pulled away.

"Billie works for an oil man I know," Peter said.

"That's all right. You don't need to explain." She wondered what kind of work Billie did. Certainly not typing with those long vermilion nails.

Peter flushed. "Would you like to see a movie?"

"If you'd like. I think we've seen the ones playing here."

"That's right. I guess they haven't changed the bill yet. We could drive over to Odessa. It's a pretty night for a drive."

"All right."

They were driving through the Texas countryside and she remembered "Some Enchanted Evening" was playing on the car radio. Suddenly Peter turned to her and said, "Ruth Ellen, what do you want out of life?"

"I haven't really thought about it," and as she said it she knew that this wasn't true, she had thought about it a great deal. "I guess the same things that every woman wants."

"Such as?"

"To marry the right man and raise a family."

He was silent and then he said, "I suppose there are some happy marriages but I haven't known any."

"I've known a lot. My mother and father were happy together."

"I wish I could say the same. Sometimes I wonder if Mother's any happier with Uncle Roberto than she was with my father."

She didn't know what to answer, but she thought his mother sounded like the kind of person who couldn't be happy with anyone. "Tell me about your father," she said.

"He's a great guy. We've always gotten along. But he's not happy. It's discouraging to think that getting older doesn't necessarily give you the answers to life. When you're little you think your parents know everything. It's a shock to find they're as confused as everyone else."

"Do you know what you want?"

"I once thought I did." He did not elaborate. "Now I'm not sure. Let's say that I'm not as idealistic as I once was."

"You sound bitter."

"Perhaps."

"I've always believed that most people are basically good. Don't you?"

"I think that everyone has his price. We all sell out somewhere along the line."

Now, thinking back, she tried to find the reasons for his bitterness, to fill in the blank spaces of what he had not told her. She had never known what went on within his mind and she wondered if that was what had made him so fascinating.

"I feel very comfortable with you," he told her. Was it that all his life people had expected too much of him? She never demanded anything. It was enough for her just to be with him, to wait for his calls. Sometimes she didn't hear from him for weeks, and then he would suddenly show up without any explanation, as if he knew that she would be there. Waiting.

And so things drifted along, and then one night he suddenly asked her to marry him. At the time it never occurred to her that he had not mentioned a very important word: love. No, he had never told her he was in love with her. He had just said, "Will you marry me?"

"Are you sure you want to?" she had asked, afraid he might change his mind.

"I'm sure."

They got a license and were married in the courthouse several days later. He had not invited his family, and she had no family to invite.

"We'll take a honeymoon trip later," he promised, but later never came.

She had never gone on a trip with him. They bought the house, she became pregnant, and their life settled into a routine. And now, less than a year later, it had all ended. . . .

❖

"Here you are." Peter's father handed her a drink and sat down on the sofa beside her.

"Thank you." She took a quick gulp.

"Too strong?"

"No." She traced the Princeton crest on the glass and wondered what to say to this man, this man whose son she had loved so desperately and tried to make happy, but there were no words to comfort either of them, and silence lay heavy between them. Then they both started to speak at the same time.

"Go ahead," he said.

"No, it wasn't important. You were going to ask me something."

"I was wondering if you'd made any arrangements yet?"

"About the . . ."

"Yes."

"I spoke to the minister of the Episcopal church here, and we had planned the . . . services . . . for Monday morning."

"I see."

"I haven't been able to go to . . . the funeral home. I thought when you got here. . . ."

"Yes. Yes, of course." Lathrop cleared his throat. "When is Peter's mother arriving?"

Ruth Ellen noticed a slight twitching of his lips and a vein in his forehead throbbed.

"A cable just came. She'll be here tomorrow."

"Is she coming alone?"

"I believe so."

There was a long pause, and then the doorbell chimed and Tornado started barking loudly.

"I expect that's the sheriff," she said.

"I'll get it." Lathrop went to the door.

More questions, going over and over it all endlessly, keeping the wounds fresh forever. Ruth Ellen thought of the newspaper clipping she had destroyed and wondered if Peter's father had known Valerie Blair. It was a question she could never ask.

"Evenin', ma'am."

"Hello, Sheriff Mahoney. Please sit down."

"Much obliged." He took off his hat and looked around for an ashtray.

"Will you need me for anything? Because if you don't I think I'll lie down a bit. I'm not feeling too well."

"Go right ahead, ma'am. I just want to talk to Mr. Spaulding here. You take it easy."

"Then please excuse me."

She went in the bedroom and lay listlessly on the bed. The voices in the next room became a distant buzz, farther and farther away, until finally she slept.

TWELVE

"Did you find out anything useful from the father?" the deputy asked.

"Not really," Sheriff Mahoney said. "A couple of names I'm going to check out. A girl young Spaulding was engaged to back in Washington, a senator's daughter."

"Oh?" The deputy looked interested. "Which senator?"

"Blair, Everitt Blair, Republican from Delaware."

"A rival enters the picture."

"It appears Spaulding and the girl broke up before he left for Midland. I doubt if she knows much. On the other hand, she might shed some light on acquaintances he had back there, what made him come out to Midland in the first place."

"Why did he?" the deputy asked.

"Same reason as most of these Yalies. Adventure, chance to strike it rich in oil."

"But I thought he came from a wealthy family."

"The money's apparently all tied up in a trust. Strings to it, so to speak. That's what those rich Easterners do, it keeps everything under control," the sheriff said.

"What's the girl's name?"

"Valerie."

"Pretty name."

"Pretty girl, so I'm told."

"Think we'll find who killed Peter Spaulding?"

"The good Lord willing and the creek don't rise."

❖

She hadn't realized it was nearly seven-thirty and she had to be at the theatre by eight. I'd better hurry, Valerie thought. She grabbed her script and a sweater and quickly walked down the stairs of the Lake Hopatcong Inn, where she was staying for the summer. In the lobby an elderly couple was playing checkers and several small children worked on a puzzle while their mother read a movie magazine nearby.

"There must be a piece missing," one whined, wiping his runny nose on his sleeve.

"No, there isn't. Just look for it, Melvin," said his mother, absorbed in Lana Turner's latest romance.

"I'm tired of doing this stupid puzzle anyway."

A handful of pieces landed on the rug.

"Melvin, you pick those up!"

"I won't."

"You do as I say or I will be very angry!" The pages of the movie magazine rustled but Melvin's mother did not stir from her chair.

"Oh, Miss Blair!" A plump lady in a print dress rushed up to Valerie. "I just loved you in *The Glass Menagerie*. You took off your part real good."

"Thank you very much."

"Would you autograph my program for me? It's in my room. I'll just go get it."

"I'd love to, but I'm on my way to the theatre now and I'm late. Will you bring it to me tomorrow?"

"Of course, dear." She lowered her voice. "Is it true that Gladys Walker was drunk opening night and they almost had to close the play?" She smacked her lips in anticipation of a choice tidbit to take back to the girls in Passaic.

"There's not a word of truth in that," Valerie said, and wondered why she was defending Gladys Walker, but stories like that going around the lake could hurt their box office.

She started toward the door and noticed a pile of New York newspapers that had just arrived. She glanced at the headlines to see what was happening in the Alger Hiss trial and suddenly froze. Halfway down the front page there was a photograph of Peter Spaulding and the caption: WASHINGTON SOCIALITE MURDERED IN TEXAS.

No! No, it couldn't be true. Not Peter. She read the details as if in a trance, not believing the printed words. Her dream of the night before last came back to her. Allowing for the difference in time, the hour that Peter was killed was the exact time he appeared in her room to tell her goodbye.

Her throat felt dry. She tried to swallow and couldn't.

Always she had pictured Peter coming back from Texas and walking into her dressing room where she was starring in a Broadway play, and things would continue as they had before, what had happened would be washed out. Someday she would tell him what she discovered after he left, what she had too much pride to write him about. For he must come back, not because he felt obligated, but because he wanted to. She had started to write him, and then she had torn up the letter. Not that way, she thought. I don't want him that way.

So he had married someone else in Texas, as a soldier stationed in a foreign land will marry out of loneliness and regret it later.

What had happened was her fault.

And fragments of the past returned, the summer night was filled with images drifting across the lake; it was winter over two years ago, the night Peter asked her to marry him. . . .

❖

New Year's Eve. The bare branches of the trees glittered like crystal chandeliers against the black sky and the ground was covered with freshly fallen snow. The fountains in front of the Comtesse de Laage's estate on Woodley Road had frozen and huge drifts of snow were piled alongside the white gravel driveway.

"We'll see what the party's like," Peter said. "If it's too stuffy we can always leave and go out to the Chevy Chase Club."

The Comtesse de Laage was one of the leading Washington hostesses. Originally from Pittsburgh where her father still drove a taxi, she had married her way up the social ladder and cut all ties with the past. Her parties were elegant and invitations sought after.

"Mother and Uncle Roberto are coming," Peter said, "but we can avoid them."

"My father's coming too," Valerie said.

"That's what I mean. I think she's having mostly older people. Not that Mother wants to be thought of as old."

"Your mother must have been very young when she married your father."

"Eighteen."

The same age as I am now, Valerie thought.

The ballroom was decorated with blue and silver balloons and Valerie noticed several friends of her father's waltzing around the floor with their wives.

"Shall we dance?" Peter asked.

"I'd love to."

"That's a beautiful dress. You look like the Snow Princess."

"I remember reading that story when I was a little girl, but I've forgotten how it ended. Did the Snow Princess live happily ever after?"

"Now that I've brought it up, I don't remember either, but I'm sure she did. By the way, do you know that old general who's giving you the eye?"

Valerie looked over Peter's shoulder. "Yes, I've met him at the house." She smiled at the general. "He's been trying to get Father to pass a bill about arms appropriations. The other senators are against it."

"Win the war and lose the peace. I wonder when we'll learn. For a while I used to think I wanted to be a diplomat, but I changed my mind."

The orchestra changed to another melody.

"Oh, that's a song I heard in Paris when I was there during the war," Peter said.

"What's it called?"

"'*J'attendrai*'."

"That means 'I will wait.'"

"Yes. The words are beautiful. Listen. . . ."

"I like it," she said.

"I'll get you a record of it."

They went to the bar for champagne. There weren't many young people at the party, Valerie noticed. And then through the doorway came a stunning dark-haired woman in a red lace Dior gown and she recognized Peter's mother. Peter had seen her too.

"Let's leave," he said. "Marcia's out at the Chevy Chase Club with a group of people. We can join them. This party's kind of dull anyway." He steered her toward the door.

"Do you see our hostess?"

Lily de Laage was standing in the entrance hall talking to the French Ambassador and his wife.

"It was a beautiful party," Valerie said. "Thank you so much."

"Oh, must you leave so soon?" The skin on the Comtesse's face was smooth and unlined from a recent face-lift, but her neck was wrinkled like a turkey's above her diamond necklace.

"Unfortunately we have to go on to another party," Peter said. "I wish we could stay longer. Thank you again."

They got in Peter's car. "I went to school with her son," Peter said. "He's a screaming fag."

"Do you think she knows?"

"It's pretty obvious to everyone else." He thought for a moment. "I wonder if a mother ever suspects that about her own son. I guess she's been too busy changing husbands to notice."

The car skidded slightly. She gasped.

"It's all right. You're not worried about my driving, are you?"

"No, but the streets are awfully icy."

"I'll go slowly."

They arrived at the Chevy Chase Club to find a wild party in progress.

"Happy New Year, pal!" A man wearing a silly hat and covered with streams of confetti slapped Peter on the back.

"Who's he?" Valerie whispered.

"Never seen him before. He must be someone's guest. Let's see if we can find Marcia in this crowd."

They greeted familiar faces, many of them bleary-eyed and unsteady on their feet.

"Hi, Valerie, Peter. Where were you two? It's almost midnight."

"At another party," Peter said. "Oh, there's Marcia."

Marcia was sitting on the stairs with a man whom she introduced as Count Miklos Szabo. "Miklos is from Budapest," she said.

Miklos stood up, giving Valerie a look of interest. "May I get you both some champagne?"

"Thank you."

Valerie and Peter sat on the steps beside Marcia.

"How was the Comtesse de Laage's party?" Marcia asked. "Was it fun?"

"Kind of stuffy," Peter said. "Mostly older people. And Mother and Uncle Roberto arrived, so we decided that was time to leave."

"You can't call this stuffy," Marcia said, as a glass smashed on the floor.

"Who's your friend?" Peter asked.

"Miklos? I just met him tonight. He's Hungarian."

"That much I gathered."

Valerie could see that Marcia was obviously intrigued by Miklos and Peter seemed to have taken an instant dislike to him. She wondered why.

Miklos returned with two glasses of champagne. "I almost had to fight a duel for these," he said.

All of a sudden the lights went out and the orchestra started to play "Auld Lang Syne."

Peter pulled her to him and kissed her. "I love you," he whispered. It was the first time he had told her.

The lights suddenly went on. Valerie noticed that Marcia's lipstick was smeared and she wondered about her own. Peter took out a handkerchief and wiped his lips.

"Let's dance," he said.

"Just a minute." Valerie pulled out her compact.

"You look fine," he said. "Come on."

He held her close on the dance floor. "I meant what I said on the steps. I'm crazy about you."

"Are you?"

"You knew I loved you."

"I wasn't sure. You never said so in all this time."

They danced a few more dances and then Peter said, "Let's leave. This has turned into a drunken brawl."

They drove back to Valerie's house.

"Do you think your father's home yet from the Comtesse's party?" Peter asked.

"I don't see his car."

They went in the living room.

"Would you like a drink?" Valerie asked.

"No thanks. I just want to be alone with you." He pulled her into his arms on the sofa and turned out the light. "You haven't said how you feel about me." He kissed her. "Do you love me?"

"Yes. Yes, I do."

"Enough to marry me?"

"Yes."

"I never thought I could be this happy," Peter said.

"Nor I."

"Suppose I'd never met you?"

"You'd have married some other girl and probably been happy. They say we don't miss what we haven't known."

"Would you have been happy with someone else?"

"No. I could never imagine loving anyone but you."

"I'll always love you," Peter said.

They did not hear the front door open, but suddenly the living room lights were switched on and Valerie's father stood there, an angry expression on his face.

"Good evening, Senator Blair," Peter said, quickly jumping up.

"Valerie, I want to speak to you. Alone." He glared at Peter. "Good night, young man."

"But, Father, we—"

"I don't care to hear any explanations."

"But, sir, we weren't doing anything wrong."

"I'll be the judge of that. Goodnight." Senator Blair pointed to the front door.

"I'll call you tomorrow, Valerie. Goodnight, sir." Peter left, casting Valerie a worried look.

"Father, how could you behave like that?" Valerie was near tears.

"I think you are the one whose behavior is in question. You know perfectly well it is improper to entertain a young man in a darkened living room with no one at home."

"But we weren't doing anything wrong."

"So young Spaulding informed me. You don't know men as well as I do, my dear. Sometimes things happen, in spite of the best intentions. One should not give them the opportunity to happen."

"I love Peter. He wants to marry me."

"I see." Senator Blair cleared his throat, as if preparing for a speech on the floor of the Senate. "I think I should inform you that sometimes men say things they don't mean when they are . . . uh . . . hoping to gain advantages."

"Oh, Father—"

"And how long had you been alone with this young man before I returned?"

"His name is Peter, and he had just brought me home."

"And you were thanking him for a nice evening?"

"I won't listen to this anymore!" Valerie started from the room, then turned. "I can understand now why Adele ran off and got married. I don't blame her for wanting to get away. This house is like a prison!" She saw an expression on her father's face as if she had slapped him.

"It's not easy to raise two daughters without a mother. And with the pressure of my work in the Senate, I haven't been able to spend as much time with you as I'd have liked."

Valerie went over and kissed him on the cheek. "I'm sorry, Father. I didn't mean what I said, but you made me angry when you implied you didn't trust me."

"I'm just trying to protect you, my dear." His voice sounded weary and old.

"I know. Goodnight, Father."

No one can protect anyone, she thought now, looking back. Because the thing her father feared would happen, finally did.

❖

The doctor had no face. Only a voice behind a white sheet hanging halfway across the operating table and her feet in stirrups, cold, cold on her bare feet. Cold steel penetrating her. The sound of a train going by, shaking the office. The heavy-set nurse holding her shoulders, wiping the perspiration from her face.

"Isn't he going to use an anesthetic?"

"It won't take long, dearie."

Scraping. Scraping. Her insides being scraped out. A life that would never be.

That night two months ago before he left.

"If you love me as much as I love you, it isn't wrong."

Scraping. Sometimes the instrument pierces the wall of the uterus. Peritonitis. A body of a girl found in an alley. No identification.

"Ow!"

"Try not to move, dearie."

Someday I'll tell him. Maybe. Years from now when it's all over and we're together. No, it would make him feel guilty. It was my fault as much as his. He must never know.

"You don't love me enough, Valerie."

"But I do. I do."

The rain. Scent of hyacinths in the wet earth. Peter gone.

He'll come back. He'll see things my way.

A missed period. A letter written and torn up. Hot baths. Steaming hot baths and gin. Another period missed. A name scrawled on a piece of paper. Cash only. Over the Maryland state line. The dirty office.

"Sit down, dearie. The doctor will see you shortly." A lascivious leer. "How far along are you?"

"Two months."

The sheet. The white sheet. She must never be able to identify him, only his voice, his voice with a faint Southern accent coming from behind the sheet, the voice that wielded the cold steel instrument.

"Would it have been a boy or a girl?" Why do I ask? What does it matter?

"It's too early to tell."

Yes. Better not to know. Blood and flesh, shapeless, formless. Nothing. Like cutting out a tumor. A bloody mass that must be cut out. Don't think about it. It has no life. Life begins at birth. It will never be born.

Another train passing.

"We're finished."

Strong arms lifting her from the table. Nausea sweeping over her.

"I think I'm going to be sick."

A pan held under her chin. Green and yellow waves dancing before her eyes. Smell of oilcloth and blood. A sharp pain and the room whirling.

"Better have her lie down for a while."

A brown leather sofa, the leather cracked and stained. A pillow under her head.

"You'll feel better in a little while, dearie."

Yes. It's over. Blood flowing again. Sharp cramps in her stomach. And an empty feeling. How empty she felt.

"I think I'm all right now."

"Are you sure?"

"Yes." I must get out of this place.

"Here are some white pills. Take them three times a day for a week."

"What are they for?"

"To dry up the milk."

"Oh."

"Don't forget to take them. And no intercourse for a month."

Valerie gave an incredulous laugh that suddenly turned to tears.

"There, there." The nurse patted her. "Are you sure you're all right?"

"Yes."

"Are you sure you can walk to your car? I don't want to walk out of here holding you up. It might look strange. The police, you know. We have to be careful."

"Yes, I can walk."

A hot blast of air. Steam rising from the pavement. The suffocating humidity of early summer. A life begun and ended. Seasons changing, years passing. Forget, Valerie. Forget.

THIRTEEN

*A*s the plane flew on through the night leaving Roberto and Rio far behind, Nina tried to sleep, but sleep would not come. Only memories, like a series of pictures in an album, recording the years, the changes that she had not noticed until after they had taken place and her children were lost to her, and she could not point to the exact moment it happened.

Peter sleeping in the nursery, moonlight streaming across his crib, the peaceful look on his baby face, his brown teddy bear clutched in his arms. Peter in knickers, sitting on a pony in Rock Creek Park, posing for a picture. Peter at Miss Hawke's Friday afternoon dancing class, the boys in dark suits and the little girls in organdy frocks and white gloves. She could see again the buxom Miss Hawke blowing her whistle for order. . . .

"Will you please get your partners and line up for the Grand March? Let's see if you remember anything from last week."

The shrill sound of the whistle again.

"Boys! Where are you going? Now . . . will the gentlemen move forward one step. I said a step—not ten! All right. Please pay attention and see how nicely you can do it. Starting with the left foot . . . one, two, three, four."

Miss Hawke's twin sister started to play the piano.

"And a double with the left, a double with the right. Shame on you! You should see the third grade do that. Take your hands out of your pockets! Now—a double to the left, a double to your right . . . Andrew, please take your hands out of your pockets! Now, back to the way we began. Come in, boys. *Hands out of your pockets!* Go—a double with your left. Take your partners and give each other your names. All right, gentlemen, face the center. Stop it! Turn around . . . position. All right, ready . . . no talking now. All right, here we go—music. Go!"

Miss Hawke wiped her perspiring red face with a handkerchief.

"A double to the left, a single, a double to the right . . . and remember, no talking through instruction! A double to the left. . . ."

The only part Peter liked about Miss Hawke's dancing class was the refreshments. Fruit punch and chocolate-covered leaves from Hubert's.

After Miss Hawke's the children went on to Mrs. Shippen's Friday night dancing class. By then Peter was attending Saint Alban's School for Boys near the National Cathedral. He was always the handsomest boy in his class, but his marks were so low he barely managed to graduate. He was bright, but he had no interest in his studies. Then he went off to Andover, until he was kicked out for that stupid episode with the waitress. She managed to get him into Lawrenceville and Lathrop donated money for their new science building. From prep school to a brief time at Princeton, and then the war. Peter in the uniform of a second lieutenant with crossed flags on his lapels. The last picture he had taken. . . .

How quickly the years had flown! And where had she gone wrong? How could they have prevented what happened?

His father could have done something, been some guiding influence during Peter's teens, but he was too busy with his chorus girls. No, she could not put the blame on Lathrop. They had all been too busy.

The communication lines had been broken long ago.

The child that inhabits our womb becomes a stranger, a stranger wandering dark streets we do not know, can never know. Too late the church bell tolls. In some forgotten city the memory of laughter, violins in a garden, life passing. Where, at some remembered moment, would we have reached out to arrest time? For time is fleeing on winged feet, mocking us when we are happy, saying: "I will give you so much and then I will take it away."

Hours of joy will be paid in bitter coin. The pendulum, ever swinging. Roses in the morning dew, now shriveled and brown with petals dropping. The golden butterfly dead on the grass. The oriole that sings no more. All passes.

Peter, my baby. Scent of talcum powder and happy gurgling sounds. Skin like rose petals wrapped in flannel. A rubber duck floating in the tub. Toy soldiers lined up on a shelf. The real soldier, grave and solemn, facing death on a foreign field. The hero's return, and then the let-down. Life's games seem tame now, after war. Shots in the night, blood sticky in the rain. Death found you after all.

Down below lie cities, towns, mountains, rivers flowing to the sea, and people living, dying. There is a beginning and end for all of us, no matter where. We cannot choose our birth, but can we choose our death? Is there a path we follow leading to a certain end? And somewhere, along the way, could we have taken a different turn toward a different end?

The plane soared on through the dark and Nina found no answer.

An old rancher in a crumpled, dust-covered suit sat in the lobby of the Scharbauer Hotel picking his teeth with the end of a matchstick. Lathrop walked up to the desk and put down his suitcase.

"I'd like a room," he said.

"Reservation?" The clerk scrutinized him.

"No."

"I'll see what we have. For how long?"

"I'm not sure yet. About a week."

The rancher put the match behind his ear, removed his hat and scratched the back of his head, never taking his eyes off Lathrop.

The clerk indicated a register blank. "Please sign here, Mister. . . ."

"Spaulding. Lathrop Spaulding."

Several heads turned and stared. The rancher pulled out his watch, wound it, and put it back in his pocket. Carefully he adjusted the tilt of his brim over his wizened, sunburned face. He looked at the door and then back at Lathrop.

The evening's entertainment in this town, thought Lathrop. Watching strangers come in and register at the hotel. He wanted to go in the bar for a drink. No, he'd have something sent to his room. He wondered if the hotel had room service. Then he remembered that Texas was a dry state. You had to carry your own bottle with you.

A Mexican bellboy took his suitcase and they went up in the elevator. Once inside the room, Lathrop took out a twenty-dollar bill.

"There's something I'd like you to get me."

The boy's eyes gleamed at the sight of the money. "A woman?"

"No. A drink. I'd like a bottle of Scotch."

"I find for you. I be back soon."

Lathrop took his shaving kit out of his suitcase and put it in the bathroom. He stared at his face over the basin, the puffiness around his eyes, he noticed how gray his hair looked, the sagging jowls, the roll of fat around his waist. His hands were trembling as he tore the cellophane wrapping off a glass, filled it with water, and swallowed his pill. He mustn't forget to take his pills. As long as he took the pills he wasn't apt to have an attack. He could lead a normal life, the doctor said. What was normal, anyway? And where was that boy with the Scotch? He wanted a drink right now, not a couple of hours from now. He needed a shave, but he'd do that in the morning.

Nina would be here in the morning. He wondered how she looked these days. Nina would never be old, no matter what happened to her. She had that kind of bone structure, the beauty that was ageless. She would look tired and pale, no doubt, but still beautiful. And he must not feel pity for her, because that was the most dangerous emotion of all, the most binding. It was easier to hate the taunting, arrogant Nina, the one who had betrayed him with another man, than the tearful, suffering Nina.

God, he felt tired! He had never felt so tired, so completely beaten by life.

You were right, Mother. Everything you said came true. She was all the things you said she was.

It was seven years since his mother's death. Every now and then, in a bus or in an elevator, he would catch the scent of Parma violets, the perfume his mother always wore, and he would turn, remembering, to see an elderly woman. He had always been sensitive to smells.

His mother was past forty when he was born. No doubt she had despaired of ever having a child. His father died when he was three and he had no memory of him. As he looked back now, he realized that his mother had been a recluse. There were no happy childhood parties, no friends coming over to play, just the two of them, mother and son. His mother always seemed to have some vague kind of illness. There were a lot of servants around, and later on, when his mother's eyesight was failing from glaucoma, a companion who read Keats to her by the hour.

His mother had taken an instant dislike to Nina when he brought her for tea. He wondered now whether it was Nina, or if it would have been any girl he wanted to marry.

But she had been fond of Peter and Marcia. And Peter, especially, was devoted to her. He used to pick bouquets of flowers and bring them to her. He had been very upset by her death.

Lathrop lay on the bed and turned on the ceiling fan. The room was suffocating. He took off his tie and unbuttoned his shirt. Better. One went through the motions of living in the midst of death. He remembered that he hadn't eaten anything since breakfast. He hadn't wanted to ask Ruth Ellen to fix dinner for him, she had looked on the point of collapse, poor little thing. She was really very sweet. Not his type, but Peter must have seen something in her.

He heard a knock on the door.

"Come in."

The bellboy entered with a bottle of Scotch, two glasses, and a container of ice. He put them on the bureau.

"You sure you not want anything else?" he asked.

"That's all."

"You change your mind, you just ring. Ask for Manuel."

Miserable little pimp. The last thing he wanted now was a woman. Lathrop opened the bottle and poured himself a stiff drink.

With numb fingers, Valerie applied grease paint to her face wondering how she was going to get through tonight's performance. Her mind was blank except for one line: WASHINGTON SOCIALITE MURDERED IN TEXAS.

Black on white. Huge black letters on dirty white paper, blotting out everything else, whirling her through black caverns. White tombstones on black snow. A black train crawling through fields of white lilies.

Death, wearing a white sheet, faceless, nameless, icy fingers reaching out.

"Fifteen minutes, Valerie."

Hurry. The curtain will be going up. You must go on and act as if nothing has happened. An audience is waiting out there in the dark beyond the footlights. They have come to live for a few hours in the world of illusion. You must give them that illusion. Only the role you are playing is real.

"Five minutes, Valerie."

"I'm ready."

Think only of your part. You are no longer Valerie. You are Laura, crippled, frightened of life, polishing your glass animals, the tiny animals that are your world. There is the music, drifting across the alley of a St. Louis tenement on a hot summer night.

The play is starting. . . .

❖

"For nowadays the world is lit by lightning! Blow out your candles, Laura—and so goodbye. . . ."

Valerie blew out the candles as the curtain fell. There was deafening applause. I got through it, she thought. You can do anything if you set your mind to it. She had not been aware of the audience or herself. She was Laura, every breath, every gesture, her crippled leg in a brace clumping across the floor. Tonight she had really lived her part.

The cast lined up for curtain calls.

"You were great tonight, kid," whispered the actor who played the Gentleman Caller.

"Thank you."

The curtain went up again and now she could see the audience applauding wildly. She remembered that there had been some discussion about *The Glass Menagerie* being too serious for summer stock, that audiences only wanted to see light comedies.

The curtain fell and Gladys Walker remained on stage to take single bows.

"At least the old gal's sober tonight," said the actor who played her son. "Last night her breath almost knocked me down."

There was a final cast curtain call and then the house lights went on.

"It proves what I've always said," announced Gladys Walker,

waving her chiffon-draped arm majestically. "People are hungry for really *good* theatre."

Valerie slipped into her dressing room and started to remove her make-up. There was a rap on the door.

"It's Matt. Are you decent?"

"Yes. Come in."

"I just wanted to tell you that whatever you did tonight, keep it up." He suddenly noticed tears in her eyes. "Anything wrong?"

"No."

"You're sure? Anything you want to tell old Uncle Matt?"

Valerie shook her head. "I'll be all right."

"I'm a good listener."

"It's just ... well, I heard some bad news about someone ... someone I used to know."

"A guy?"

She nodded. "I'm fine now." She took a tissue and wiped off her mascara. She forced a smile. "It was all over a long time ago."

"Okay. We'll see you at the Blue Boar."

"Not tonight, Matt."

"Come on. A few laughs will do you good."

"I couldn't. Really. Besides, I have to study my lines for next week."

"Whatever you say."

She continued to remove her make-up. I'm all right, she told herself. It happened a long time ago. It was a long time ago and I got over it. A long time ago. . . .

Peter and Valerie had gone with another couple to the Glen Echo Amusement Park in Maryland. It was late June and the night was hot and sticky. They had been on the roller coaster and the carousel, the boats on the lake, and the fun house. Valerie was eating a pink cotton candy cone.

"Oh, look! Let's go in and have our fortunes told." She pointed to a sign: MADAME OLGA.

"They're all fakes," Peter said.

"I heard she was good. Come on."

Madame Olga was sitting at a table covered with a purple fringed cloth on which was a crystal ball and a pack of cards. She was about sixty with heavy Slavic features and she wore a black dress and large gold earrings.

"You would like a reading?" she asked.

"Yes," Valerie said, glancing at Peter.

"Please sit down." Madame Olga indicated the chair opposite her. "And the gentleman over there." She picked up the cards and shuffled them. Valerie noticed that her fingernails were dirty under the peeling red polish. She handed Valerie the cards. "Make a wish and cut the cards three times." She closed her eyes and mumbled something in Russian.

"Ah, very good cards." Madame Olga picked up the cards and spread them out in a pattern, seven to a row. "Most interesting. Much activity around you. Crowds of people. I see you...." Madame Olga closed her eyes. "You are always surrounded by people, yet always alone." She peered at Valerie over the crystal ball. "You dance, no?"

"Yes, I do dance, but...."

"Parties, yes, I see many parties. You have many friends. But there is something else. There is a curtain. It opens and closes and I hear applause."

"Yes, that is what I would like to do."

"And you will." She picked up the King of Diamonds. "I see a man with white hair. Much older. He speaks in a hall before other men. I think he is related to you."

"My father."

Madame Olga nodded. "He loves you very much. He worries about you." She fingered the Seven of Clubs. "A message in a short time from a lady. Like a letter. Yes, it is a letter. It comes from across water."

"From my sister?"

"Yes. It is from your sister. She has something to tell you. It will arrive in a few days." Madame Olga picked up the Ten of Clubs. "A journey. Are you planning a journey?"

"No."

"Then it must be your sister who is coming here."

"Maybe." Valerie looked dubious.

"I get a message from someone in the spirit world. A lady. She says that she is watching over you. She is happy there."

"My mother."

"She says to tell your father not to blame the doctors. Her time was up. Do you understand what she means?"

"Yes." Valerie suddenly felt goose pimples on her arms.

"I see for you many invitations, many proposals. You will travel much in your lifetime. You have a long life, good health. Success in what you want to do."

Madame Olga stopped talking. Apparently the reading was over.

"You didn't say anything about marriage," Valerie said.

"Oh." Madame Olga gathered up the cards. "You will be married. Three times." She shuffled them rapidly. "Now, the young man would like me to read his future?"

"I don't think so," Peter said.

"Please. I want to hear what Madame Olga has to say about you."

"All right." Peter sat down opposite Madame Olga and cut the cards. The first card was the Ace of Spades. Then the Queen of Spades and the Ten of Clubs.

Madame Olga opened her eyes and they had a strange expression. She seemed to be choosing her words carefully.

"There is a journey for you. You will move to another place. It is west of here, flat country." She spread out the cards. "There is danger involved in your work. You must be careful. Someone will be jealous of you." Madame Olga appeared to be breathing heavily. "I see a lady asking you not to go, but you will go anyway." She took out a handkerchief and mopped her brow. "The messages I am getting are not clear. I hear a man's voice. He says he knew you in Italy. Does that mean anything? He says to remember the monastery."

Peter's look of disbelief turned to one of amazement.

"That is all I get. I have been doing so many readings. It is the heat."

Peter took out his wallet and handed her a ten-dollar bill. He took Valerie's arm and they went outside.

"She gave me the creeps," Valerie said.

"I still say she's a fake," Peter said. "Let's find Gloria and Brad. It's getting late."

Valerie noticed that his face was pale.

It was the following April that he left for Texas, and the lady Madame Olga had seen asking him not to go was herself. And, just as she predicted, he went anyway, and she never saw him again.

She felt icy cold and empty inside. Tonight's applause echoed in her ears with a hollow ring. Always surrounded by people, yet always alone. Was that her future?

FOURTEEN

S aturday. Another morning of waking with Peter gone, the empty space in the bed, the harsh reality of the days ahead. Wearily, Ruth Ellen dragged herself out of bed. Today Peter's mother was arriving. Today she would meet the woman of whom he had spoken so little, except in bitterness, the woman who had set the pattern of all women for him, the woman whose love and approval he had wanted and never had.

She started to dress, and an incident came back to her, the first time she and Peter had guests for dinner. . . .

She prided herself on her cooking. It was something she could do really well, and she had arranged the table so that it looked especially pretty. She had copied the centerpiece from a picture in a magazine, an arrangement of red and white carnations in a copper bowl.

No sooner had they sat down to dinner than Peter's eyes began to water and he seemed to have difficulty breathing.

"Is anything the matter?" she asked, worried.

He was staring at the flowers. "No," he said.

That night he had an attack of asthma, the first since he was a child. He told her later that his mother always wore a perfume with a carnation base. It brought back the evenings after she divorced his father, when she would come in his room dressed to go out and kiss him goodnight. There was the feel of chiffon brushing his cheek as she bent over him and the strong scent of carnations.

"Where are you going, Mummy?"

"To a party, darling. Now go to sleep."

"No. I don't want you to go."

"You're mussing my dress. Be a good boy."

"Who are you going out with?"

"A friend."

"I hate him!"

He told Ruth Ellen how he stood at the window and watched his mother drive off into the night with Roberto Carvalho, hearing her laughter, and then the spasms would start, the choking, and Fräulein would plug in the vaporizer and force steam into his lungs. He used to imagine himself dying during one of the attacks and his mother dressed in black at his funeral, weeping. She would be sorry, she would really be sorry. His mouth was twisted as he said this, his eyes again those of the hurt, lonely little boy, and Ruth Ellen swore to herself to make it all up to him. Over and over again she told him how much she loved him. He seemed not to hear, he was lost in the past, unforgiving, wanting what had never been, could never be.

The sad, lost child in Peter was what she had loved, she wanted to protect and mother him, to drive away the dark clouds she saw in his eyes, she wanted him to need her. If he needed her enough, he would never leave her.

He had left her anyway.

She brushed her hair back and tied it with a ribbon. In the mirror she saw that there were deep blue shadows under her eyes and her face was pinched and drawn. She looked at Peter's photograph in his uniform and she remembered the night he told her about the war.

"We came ashore at Salerno," he said, "and we fought our way up to Rome. Eight months it took us, eight bloody, grueling months.

You've heard of sunny Italy? Well, so had I. Sunshine and olive groves and all that sort of thing. They don't tell you about the rain, how the valleys turn into seas of black mud, what it's like sloshing through it kneehigh. Sometimes we went as long as two weeks without being able to take off our shoes and get our feet dry.

"We fought in the mountains that winter, sleeping at night behind rocks with the temperature below freezing and snow sifting over us. My job was to string the communication lines without being hit by German artillery or rocks. Every time there was an artillery barrage there was danger of flying rocks. Those big boulders sounded like a windstorm coming down the mountainside, and when you heard that sound you got out of the way—fast. A lot of guys couldn't move fast enough. In one battalion they had more casualties from rock slides than German bullets.

"We were grimy and dirty and unshaven, the officers as well as the men. The few times we were able to shave and clean up we were such a sickly white we looked like patients in a hospital ward.

"The only thing that kept up our morale was our company commander, Captain Ernie Flather. He was the kind of guy the men would do anything for. I don't think I've ever known any man as loved and respected. He was gentle and sincere, with a sense of humor and real guts. Ernie was a Texan from Wichita Falls. His father was the postmaster there. . . ."

Peter paused, as if the rest was too painful to tell.

"On the road to Rome there was a town called Cassino, with heavily fortified mountains behind it. On one peak sat an old Benedictine monastery. The Germans had control of it and were firing down on us. We got orders to take the monastery.

"We started up the mountain. It was a hopeless task. They were just picking us off. Somehow I managed to get back. Ernie didn't. That night they brought the dead men down the slopes lashed to the backs of mules. It was an eerie sight. The moon was almost full and you could see the bodies lying belly-down across the wooden packsaddles, their legs sticking out stiffly on one side and their heads hanging over the other side, bobbing up and down as the mules walked. Like rag dolls. That morning they had been men. I thought how I could have been one of them. I waited for Ernie.

"Finally I saw him. Or what had been Ernie. Two men unlashed his body from the mule and laid him on the ground next to a stone wall. 'It's the Captain,' I heard a man say. Others gathered round. One knelt down and put his hand on Ernie's shoulder. 'God damn it,' he said. 'I sure am sorry, old man.' Ernie was twenty-seven. He had a wife and child back in Wichita Falls. He had plans for a good future and now he lay in a row of dead bodies. It was all over for Ernie. How do you figure life anyway? There were men in that company no one liked. They came back.

"Nearly four months later we entered Rome. The victors. There were cheering crowds in the streets waving flags and throwing flowers and kisses. I thought how Ernie deserved all of this, he should have been with us. Instead he was buried in a nameless grave at the foot of a mule trail.

"I looked up Ernie's family later on. They were good people. But what the hell do you say? What do you say to a broken old man whose dreams have been destroyed? To a young widow with empty eyes and a kid who doesn't understand why his daddy doesn't come back? 'Your daddy was a hero, son. You can be very proud of him. You can play with his medals.' It doesn't make up for his loss. Nothing does."

No, she thought, looking back, nothing makes up for the loss of someone you love. The soldier killed in war, the good, responsible member of the community killed in a senseless car accident; Peter, shot down by an unknown assailant. It is all the same. The void is there and the same questions asked over and over again.

Why them? Why those particular people? What had they done to deserve early, violent deaths? Why doesn't death take the bad ones instead of the good?

She thought again of her father. He had stood for right, for the law, and he was shot down by one of the lawless. And now Peter, for no reason. Or does there have to be a reason? Is one just in the wrong place at the wrong time? Would five minutes earlier or five minutes later have made a difference? Her father always knew the risks he faced and he was not afraid. She had never seen him show fear. "Someone has to uphold the law," he said. It was matter-of-fact, a statement, said without emotion, without heroics. Her father would not have considered himself a hero. He was only doing his duty. Death was his shadow, and finally, death faced him.

It's not fair, it's not fair, it's not fair, a voice within her kept repeating. Life isn't fair!

Lathrop splashed cold water in his face. The cheap whiskey had given him a hangover. That miserable little pimp had no doubt gotten it from a friend and pocketed the difference. He took the bottle and poured the rest of it down the drain. Mustn't forget his pill. It was only when he drank a lot that he sometimes forgot and had an attack. Thank God he'd never had one when he was driving. They'd take away his license if they knew.

Today he had to go to the funeral home and choose the casket and attend to all the details that Ruth Ellen had not been able to do. It was a man's job, anyway. Strange, he always thought his son would be doing it for him instead of the other way round. A son is a man's chance to see the tomorrow he will never see, to do the things he never did. He is his prayer for immortality, the runner to whom he hands his flickering torch and says, "Carry on. My race is run."

What did I bequeath you, oh my son?

Where did I fail? The years that separated us were like a sea I could not cross.

Do they separate all fathers and sons?

The helpless baby, the toddler taking his first unsteady steps across the lawn toward the outstretched arms, the small boy watching worshipfully as you show him how to untangle his fishing reel? Then, suddenly, he is the reserved adolescent, watching you with wary eyes, no longer taking your advice because he knows all the answers and you are a fool, an old fool of whom he must be tolerant.

And you say to yourself: Wait. When you have your own son you will know how I feel. Then you will come to me and say, "Dad, you were right."

You will put your arms around my neck and say. . . . Tears were rolling down his cheeks and he was trembling. There were so many talks we should have had, he thought, so much I wanted to say to you and didn't. Peter, my son, if only I could speak to you once more, to say all the things that are in my heart, to know that you understand. I did my best. I tried. I tried, but life was too much for me.

He swallowed his pill. He must get control of himself. In only a few hours Nina would be here.

❖

To Nina the flight seemed endless. They were fighting strong headwinds all the way up the coast of South America and the turbulence had made many of the passengers ill.

The buzzer sounded from the seat in back of her and the stewardess came running down the aisle with a harried look.

"My wife isn't feeling very well," said a young naval officer. "Is there anything you could give her?"

"I'll get something."

Nina could see the girl between the seats. She looked about seven months pregnant and very frightened. The plane shook violently.

The stewardess returned with the pills and a glass of water. "Here you are."

"It's our first baby," the young officer said. "My wife doesn't like flying, but we wanted our child to be born back in the United States."

The girl clung to him. She couldn't have been more than nineteen, Nina thought, and she wondered what it would be like to be that young again. Young and full of hope. Had she ever been that young?

"It's all right, darling," she heard him say. "Everything's going to be all right."

Those comforting words. How nice to be able to believe them. Everything's going to be all right. The illusions of youth. Once long ago, she too had believed those words. She tucked the blanket around her and closed her eyes. Now it all came back again . . . sharply, and with a kind of stabbing pain . . . the years of her marriage to Lathrop Spaulding.

One night especially. . . .

They had been to a party in Greenwich and Lathrop had been drinking heavily. He refused to let her drive.

"You don't think I'm drunk, do you, my darling wife?" He shoved her aside roughly. "I'm perfectly capable of driving. That's the trouble with all you women. Every one of you wants to run the show."

He took all the curves on two wheels, laughing like a maniac. She was too frightened to speak. She kept hoping a policeman would come along, but none did. By some miracle they got back to their apartment alive.

"Didn't think I'd make it, did you?"

She walked in their bedroom without answering.

He followed her and grabbed her by the shoulders. "You don't have any faith in me. Do you?"

She saw the wild eyes of a stranger.

"Answer me, you bitch!"

"Yes, of course I do." She had never seen him like this before. It was not the time to start an argument. Better to agree with him and hope he would pass out so she could get him to bed.

Suddenly, without warning, he threw back his head and let out a raucous and terrifying scream. It was guttural, like the cry of an animal, and he fell to the floor, writhing in convulsions. His face was pale and his pupils dilated, while his eyeballs rolled upward. Terrible spasms jerked his arms as if they were being twisted in their sockets and bloody foam trickled from his lips.

Epilepsy!

She stood frozen in horror, not knowing what to do. His tongue! She must see that he didn't swallow his tongue. She tried to remember what she had heard about epileptic seizures. She had never seen one before. She had no idea, he had never said anything.

His face was turning purple now. The rhythmic jerking continued, but less violently.

Slowly the spasms subsided, and his deformed features returned to normal. She took a handkerchief and wiped the foam from his mouth. His eyes were closed and he appeared to have fallen into a deep sleep.

She thought of trying to lift him onto the bed, but he was too heavy. She might pull something, bring on a miscarriage. The baby! Suddenly it occurred to her that the baby she was carrying could have inherited the disease. Instinctively, she clutched her stomach.

Oh, my God! she thought. No!

Why hadn't Lathrop said anything to her, warned her? Would she have married him if he had? Was that why he had kept silent, hoping to keep his affliction from her?

She went back in her mind over things he had said, trying to see if there had been any indications. He had mentioned having rheumatic fever as a child. That was the reason he didn't go in for sports, except for swimming, even though he had the build of a football player. It had weakened his heart, he said. As long as he was careful, there was no need to be concerned. He had to watch himself about putting on weight, that was all.

Now she realized it wasn't rheumatic fever at all, but epilepsy.

She recalled that one time she had made some casual remark about a person having fits, and Lathrop's face ... yes, his face had looked strange for a moment and he started to say something and stopped.

Had he tried to tell her?

She looked at him lying on the floor, sleeping peacefully, calmly, now that it was all over. What would she say when he awoke?

She remembered that his mother had been against their marriage, but she assumed it to be the overpossessiveness of a mother with an only son, thinking that no girl was good enough for him. Now, she realized that his mother could have had another reason. Had she thought he didn't have the right to marry? Or did she dread the day when his illness would be discovered and a woman would turn to him and say, "Why didn't you tell me?"

He should have told her. It wasn't fair that he let her marry him, not knowing.

What would she have done in his place?

She was nineteen and frightened and she didn't know where to turn. Seeing him go into a convulsion had terrified her, and now she would be waiting for others, watching him, looking for signs that he was about to have one. But there were no signs, no warnings. This attack had come on without any indication. It could have happened in the car driving home and then they would have been killed, it could have happened at a party, in front of everyone.

Tomorrow she would go to the library and read everything she could find about epilepsy. She would ask her doctor ... no, she couldn't ask him. She had heard doctors talk at parties, practically giving case histories without mentioning names. "I had an interesting case last week. A patient of mine discovered that. . . ."

She would die if this got out.

When she first became pregnant she had to fill out a form. Did anyone in your family have asthma, diabetes or epilepsy? it read. She had checked asthma because her uncle had attacks. Lathrop had seen the form but had volunteered no information. The doctor told him she was very healthy and should have an easy pregnancy.

Easy, she thought with irony.

She looked again at the figure on the floor. He was stirring.

After about an hour he awoke and she helped him to bed. He had no recollection of the attack the next morning, all he said was, "I guess I had a little too much to drink last night."

She watched him, saying nothing. He really did not remember. She wished she could forget, or else pretend it had never happened. Now she knew the truth.

She would go to the big library at Fifth Avenue and 42nd Street and go through some of the medical books. She would find out everything she could.

Four months later Peter was born. In the delivery room she kept asking the doctor over and over if he was all right.

"Fine. He's a beautiful baby."

"But is he all right?"

"Perfect. He has all his fingers and toes. Now stop worrying."

"That's not what I mean."

It was too soon to tell. Now she must wait, dreading, for signs she had read about. The vacant stare, dizzy spells, twitching. The sudden loss of control and foaming at the mouth. No, no, dear God, no. Such a beautiful baby, with deep blue eyes and long, black silky lashes and tiny, perfect features. She would watch him and guard him carefully and see that she didn't have any more children.

Peter was baptized at Saint Bartholomew's in a long white christening robe that had been worn by Lathrop and Lathrop's father before him. He was a good baby and smiled like an angel when the minister made a cross with holy water on his tiny forehead.

"Open the gate unto us who knock; that this child may enjoy the everlasting benediction of Thy heavenly washing, and may come to the eternal kingdom which Thou hast promised by Christ our Lord. Amen."

The everlasting benediction. Had Peter received that? Why had he been taken so young, without having the chance to make something of his life?

She must find some reason that she could accept for Peter's death. To accept the unacceptable. One has to come to some terms with life, she thought, or else it destroys you.

The room was filled with cockroaches, giant cockroaches crawling along the floor, climbing out of cracks in the wall. Why had they never warned her about Brazilian cockroaches? She must kill them. She must find some way to poison them before they got to Peter. They must not harm her baby. They were all around her, grinning at her with evil eyes. He was crying. She could hear Peter crying.

I must get to him. I must get to him quickly and save him.

She heard a voice, blurred, she seemed to be coming out from under ether.

"Can I get you something?"

She opened her eyes. Where was she? She could hear him crying, she must rescue him. Slowly, she realized where she was. The plane. She was on the plane. A baby was crying, but it was not Peter. It was a baby on the plane, his cries penetrating her sleep.

And Peter was dead.

FIFTEEN

*T*he smell of wet leaves and wood smoke. Red berries, their green leaves dripping with raindrops. Wet pine needles and puddles of water. A flock of crows flew to a bare oak tree and started to caw.

"Look, Daddy!"

Barking of beagles. Peter running across the fields.

A moment frozen in time.

Lathrop touched the place on his chin where he had cut himself shaving. It was bleeding again. He went in the bathroom and applied pressure with a wet washcloth.

He had not been around when Peter first started to shave. Or when he had his first drink. He was surprised when he found that Peter had started to smoke. He still saw him as a little boy.

Peter had suddenly grown up without his realizing it. The visits became less frequent and one day he was confronted by a stranger, who was his son. The price of divorce.

But it had not been his fault, he told himself. He was not the one who wanted a divorce, it was Nina. He had begged and pleaded for the sake of the children. No, for himself too. She was insistent.

Nina was the kind of woman who could leave a sinking ship without even a backward glance.

His chin had stopped bleeding. Better get going, he thought. The coroner was waiting for him at the morgue.

❖

Sheriff Mahoney studied the reports on his desk, still puzzling about the phone call. It had come shortly after he arrived at the courthouse.

"Someone wants to speak to the sheriff. She says it's personal."

"Sheriff Mahoney?" The woman's voice sounded scared.

"Speakin', ma'am."

"I have some information about Peter Spaulding's murder. Would you like it?"

"Sure would, ma'am." This could be the break they'd been waiting for. "Can you come in and talk to us?"

There was a pause and the sound of breathing "I can't. He'd kill me if. . . ." Then a click.

Sheriff Mahoney scratched his head. Still nothing to go on. No telling whether that call was the real McCoy or just another of the worthless leads they always got after every murder. Sometimes women became vindictive and wanted revenge for some reason or other. He'd seen it happen before. If young Spaulding had been involved with some dame and thrown her over . . . no, that was too simple.

Hanged if he had any ideas, but he'd better get this thing solved. Elections were coming up before too long and he aimed to go on being sheriff.

Not that an unsolved murder was anything new in these parts, it happened all the time, but the others hadn't caused any stir outside of Texas. Just another fuss that ended in a shooting, and nobody paid any attention. With this here one the Washington and New York newspapers were calling and asking questions he couldn't answer and making him look like a danged fool. Now the F.B.I. and old man Spaulding's personal investigator were in on it too.

He didn't like these rich Easterners anyhow. The way they talked in those snooty voices and looked down on people. Served them right for coming out here and messing in things that belonged to Texans. He took a wad of tobacco from his pouch and started to chew.

He felt right sorry for the wife, though. Pretty little thing, the kind he'd have liked for a daughter if he'd ever got married. Well, you couldn't waste no sympathy in the job he was in. In a way he was glad he had no family, unless you counted the kinfolk back in Pin Hook as family, and he hadn't seen them since he left there when he was eighteen. Got tired of pickin' pecans and doin' chores. His folks were dirt poor and the only girl he ever wanted to marry ran off with some city slicker.

It had been a long road from the little town of Pin Hook near the Oklahoma border to being sheriff of Midland. He'd seen this town grow in fifteen years from hardly more than a village to a good-sized city with skyscrapers. And it was his city. He was the law and he aimed to keep it that way.

Still, he'd like to get this case closed and have those danged newspaper people off his back.

Something had to break soon.

❖

She shouldn't have made that phone call, Billie Johnson told herself, it was a fool thing to do. If he ever found out she'd tried to squeal . . . she shuddered at the thought. She wondered if the sheriff could trace her call. No, she'd hung up too fast. You had to stay on the line for them to trace a call, she'd read that someplace.

It was that beating he'd given her last night that made her do it, she just couldn't take any more. But where would she go if she left him? He'd only find her and bring her back.

She would never be able to escape him. Never. She knew too much.

She tried to warn Peter, but it hadn't done any good. Funny thing was, except for the other afternoon, she'd stopped seeing Peter months ago. Oh, they'd had some fun times together when she first met him, but she knew she didn't mean anything to him, he was carrying a torch for some society girl back East. She was just someone to go to bed with, but he'd treated her decent, he was the only real gentleman she'd ever known. Nothing would have come of it, he couldn't have introduced her to his family or his fancy friends. She'd known that from the beginning. A nice kid, younger than she was, and she never intended to fall in love with him. It was just for kicks. That was how life fooled you.

If only she could pull up stakes and start another life somewhere, have a home and kids like other women, forget her past. Men didn't want to marry her, they only wanted to go to bed with her. It had been that way since she was fifteen.

You're a born loser, Billie, she told herself. The cards are stacked against you, they always have been.

Thirty. That's not old. It's not young either. In a few years I'll be too old to have kids. I'll go on singing in sleazy dives and being kept by married men, and then the men will start looking for younger dames and what's left? Carrying trays in some hash house?

Once she'd had dreams of being a movie star, when she was a little girl in Spokane where her father was a plumber. She entered all the local amateur contests and she won a trip to Hollywood and a screen test at Paramount. They put her under contract and at the end of six months dropped her. She found that being a starlet meant entertaining at stag parties, and the promised parts never materialized. She couldn't go back to Spokane a failure. She went to New York and got a job dancing at the Latin Quarter. And then she was introduced to this wealthy oil man who wanted her to come out to Texas and marry him. Only thing he didn't mention was that he already had a wife who had no intention of divorcing him. Men, she thought in disgust. They were all alike. Rotten. Except for Peter.

But he'd used her too, like all the rest. He'd married that dull little Ruth Ellen, God knows why. Just given her the brush with no explanation.

Damn them all! she thought.

It was a crazy idea to call the sheriff. Did she think she'd get a reward or something? No, all she'd get would be a bullet in the back. Better stay out of it. She'd tried to save Peter but they had gotten to him anyway.

Look out for yourself, Billie, she told herself. It's a cinch no one else will.

The grizzly business was over. The identification of his son's body lying on a slab in the mortuary. The sheet pulled back briefly, enough to see the battered face that had once contained all his hopes of immortality. THE END, carved on a tombstone, written in tears and blood.

He wanted a drink. He wanted to get so drunk that he couldn't think. He staggered out into the blinding sunlight, the steam rising from the pavements, the dry dust choking his lungs, wondering where to go, which direction to take, for all streets led nowhere now.

What did life hold for him?

What did it offer but empty days and nights stretching end on end, black caverns of despair.

Faces passed him, the blank faces of strangers, some turned and stared, he heard the twang of voices, honking of horns, he walked on.

Oblivion. Now he understood what they were seeking, those lost and lonely ones who drowned themselves in alcohol. To return to a state of peace where there is no responsibility for living, to float, as in a womb.

Eternal peace. To float endlessly. . . .

There was a sudden blast of a horn and screeching of brakes as a black Cadillac with steer horns on the front missed him by inches.

An angry red face wearing a cowboy hat leaned out the window. "Look out where y' goin', ya stupid son of a bitch!"

Lathrop opened his mouth to say something and a cloud of brown dust blew in his face as the car sped on.

He hadn't even seen it approaching. And what did it matter if it had hit him? Where was he going?

He looked around to see where he was. A few blocks ahead he saw the hotel. Nina should be arriving any time. He had to pull himself together. A shower, ice cold water splashing on him, yes, that would help, a shower and a tall cool drink.

He walked faster. Sweat poured down his face and he took off his rumpled gray seersucker jacket. His shirt was sticking to him in damp patches. He mopped his face and neck with a handkerchief. His eyelids felt grainy from specks of sand and dust. He looked at his handkerchief. Streaks of grime covered it and blood from where his chin was bleeding again. Damn! He'd better stop in a drugstore.

On the corner, waiting for the light to change, he saw a newspaper stand. He looked at the headlines. NO CLUES TO SPAULDING MURDER.

He wondered if the investigator he'd hired had come up with anything. Whoever did it could be in Mexico by now, safe from prosecution. Or he could be right here in Midland. He intended to find him if it was the last thing he ever did.

SIXTEEN

Sheriff Mahoney looked over a report that had just come from the F.B.I. in Washington. He scowled, then took out the growing file marked SPAULDING, and clipped the papers to some others. He spread out several photographs on his desk, the ones taken of the body that were too gruesome for the newspapers to publish, made a few notes on a pad, then put the pictures back in the file with the rest of the data.

"It's sure one Jim Dandy of a problem," he said.

"Are you really going to ask old man Spaulding if he'll take a polygraph test?" the young red-haired deputy asked.

"Why not?"

"You don't suspect him, do you?"

"Everyone's a suspect until proven innocent," Sheriff Mahoney said, biting off the end of a cigar and lighting it.

The deputy thought that the saying was "innocent until proven guilty," but it seemed wiser not to point this out to Sheriff Mahoney, who had a hell of a temper when he got going.

"Why would he want his own son killed?" he asked.

"I didn't say he did," the sheriff growled. "But Lathrop Spaulding is concealing something from us." He blew out a cloud of black smoke. "I aim to find out what it is."

The deputy picked up the German Luger. "Where did you find this?"

"In an army locker he had stored in his garage. Locked. There was something in it he didn't want his wife to see. She found the key in his bureau drawer and opened it. I wish we'd gotten to it first."

"Do you think she took anything out? Like letters?"

"Hard to tell. But she looked kind of funny when I asked her if that was all that was in it. Didn't seem reason enough to keep it locked."

"The gun wasn't loaded?"

"No. Probably took it off some Kraut who'd run out of ammunition. War souvenir to show the grandchildren someday."

"He seemed to like German things." He turned the pages of a book of fairy tales. "It's all written in German."

"Yeah. He had a German nurse. Those rich Easterners don't want to be bothered raising their own children."

"The poor little rich boy."

"That's about the story." Sheriff Mahoney picked up a postcard and studied it. "Pretty little town."

"Where is it?"

"Somewhere in Germany. Freudenstadt. Never heard of it." He scribbled another name on the pad in front of him: Erna Schmidt. "She's probably dead by now," he said.

Freudenstadt is a small town deep in the Black Forest, and it was here that she was born and spent her childhood before going off to America to become a governess for other people's children. Erna Schmidt, her passport read, and the photograph showed a middle-aged woman with a plain, scrubbed face and dark braids wound round her face, "Fräulein" to the children in whose homes she had lived until they grew too big to need her anymore.

And now she was back in Freudenstadt taking care of her aged mother, her mother who believed that der Führer was still alive and leading them to a glorious victory, who babbled on about the Fatherland and Hans who would return any day from Stalingrad, not realizing that Hans was dead and Germany defeated.

"Erna," came the whining voice from the next room, "Erna, read me the letter from Hans."

What use to explain again? Her mother did not understand. Hans, the youngest and favorite son, would never come home from the bloody snow at Stalingrad, but in her mother's mind he lived on, blond and handsome in his uniform with the Iron Cross, Hans, her baby, her hero.

"Erna . . . where are you?"

"I'm coming." She knew the letter by heart now. He had thought he was fighting for a great cause. Poor Hans. All of them deluded. She had seen the changes coming over her beloved Germany on her visits home, but she could understand how they looked for a new leader after the terrible times following the First World War, those times she remembered well because she was in her teens then and there was hardly enough to eat. Her parents used to send her out with Gottfried to pick berries in the woods. Hans was a baby then, and she, Erna, was the eldest. The desperate search for food, the nights they went to bed with empty stomachs, the old men, bitter, disillusioned, begging with tin cups. Gottfried went to work in Hamburg and she, finally, to America.

Years of working, sending money home, never spending any on herself, Erna Schmidt, Fräulein, in starched white uniform and cap, wheeling children in carriages, singing them German lullabies, telling them fairy tales about the Black Forest, home a small dark room with a narrow bed and bureau, dreaming of a little town with cobbled streets and church spires, of pine trees heavy with snow. . . .

"Erna, you never worked for Jews in America?" How often her mother had asked her this question.

Not far away, in Nuremburg, the war trials had just ended, yet the old hatreds lived on. How many denied knowledge of the concentration camps that existed in their midst? "I did not know what was going on." The old familiar cry. To deny guilt rather than face it, because to face it was too terrible. My poor Germany, what happened to you? How did you let these things happen?

"Erna, I want my tea."

"Coming, Mutti."

To wait on others, to never have any life of her own, was that all she could expect? What had become of the babies she raised, sent out into the world, had they forgotten her? She would never forget any of them, she kept their pictures and remembered them at Christmas and on their birthdays.

There was one especially. Little Peter. . . .

"Ach, I will take you back to Germany with me and dress you in *lederhosen*," she used to say.

"And will you take me for walks in the Black Forest and show me the gnome's house, Fräulein?"

"*Ja, mein Peter.*"

Such a handsome little boy, so affectionate and lonely. It was the worst day of her life when she had to leave him. His mother said he was too big for a governess, and he would be going off to camp in the summer anyway.

"I'll never forget you, Fräulein. You'll write to me, won't you?"

For a while there were letters, and then Christmas cards with a message. She had not heard anything in a long time. She hoped he did not hate all Germans because of the war. He must be twenty-eight years old now. It did not seem possible!

Where was he now and did he remember his old nurse? If ever she got back to America she must try and find him. Maybe he was married and had a baby she could take care of. Poor Peter, such awful asthma attacks he had, how they frightened her. To see the poor little thing choking and gasping for breath, it was enough to tear your heart out. And his mother not there half the time. How could she leave such a fine man like Mr. Spaulding? Selfish and heartless she was, thinking only of herself, not like a good German wife. If she, Erna Schmidt, had ever had a chance to marry a man such as that ... ach, why think about what was not possible.

"Erna, what are you doing?"

"Coming, Mutti."

The withered old woman sat in the bedroom, her blue eyes staring vacantly ahead. Erna took out the worn letter that had come from Stalingrad that January morning over six years ago.

Frau Schmidt smiled happily and clasped her gnarled, blue-veined hands over her stomach, slowly rocking back and forth in her chair. "Such a good boy, *mein Hans*. He never forgets to write his mother. Soon he will be home."

"Yes, Mutti." Erna started to read, barely glancing at the letter:

Liebe Mutti,

The fighting all around us has been fierce and many men have been taken prisoner by the Russians. If the airfield is still in our possession, this letter may still get out. The Führer has promised to bail us out of here, they read a message to us from him this morning, and I firmly believe it, he will not let us down. So do not worry, dear Mutti, no matter what you read in the newspapers. I am not afraid. We will be victorious for the Führer and the Fatherland.

Your loving son,
Hans

She put down the letter. Illusions. Lies. Had Hans really believed they would be rescued? She had heard of other last letters from Stalingrad, letters that had been found in the rubble and never delivered, letters that were bitter and full of despair, written by soldiers who knew they were about to die for a cause they had lost all faith in, for a leader who had betrayed them.

Was it better that Hans died still believing?

In the kitchen the kettle was whistling on the stove.

"I'll get your tea now, Mutti," she said. "The water is boiling."

SEVENTEEN

*L*athrop walked through the lobby and picked up his key at the desk. There were several messages in his box. Ruth Ellen had called while he was out and Sheriff Mahoney wanted to see him. No word yet from the private investigator he had hired. That fellow had better be on the job, he thought, for all the money he was paying him.

He started in the direction of the elevators. Was it his imagination? There was a faint scent of carnations, it lingered in the air like a mist, a perfume that could only belong to one person.

He walked back to the desk. "Has Senhora Carvalho arrived yet?" he asked the clerk.

"The Brazilian lady?"

Lathrop nodded. She's not Brazilian, he wanted to say, but why bother? "Is she here?"

"She just went up in the elevator."

"What room is Senhora Carvalho in?"

The clerk pulled a card out of the file. "Room three thirty-one."

We're on the same floor, Lathrop thought. He was perspiring again, even though the lobby was fairly cool. "Thank you," he said absently, wiping his face with his handkerchief. How long had it been since he had last seen Nina? Nine years? Ten? An instant and an eternity. He rang the bell for the elevator. The doors opened, closed. He noticed the pattern in the carpet. Why did they use such gaudy colors?

"What floor, sir?" The operator was staring at him.

"Three."

The elevator stopped with a jerk, the doors opened, he stepped out into the corridor. Three thirty-one, he thought. Two men passed him, talking loudly about an oil deal. He saw an open door and then a bellboy came out rattling some change. It was Manuel.

Lathrop passed him without speaking and stopped in front of the door. 331. He rapped on it.

"Yes?" It was her voice. "Who is it?"

"Lathrop."

The door opened and there stood Nina. Her face was pale, the skin drawn and taut across the high cheekbones, she looked fragile and helpless and as beautiful as he remembered, almost nun-like in her all black garb. Sorrow became her, as did every other role she chose to play.

"Lathrop," she said. Her voice was barely more than a whisper and tears glistened on her eyelashes. She swayed toward him and he felt the coolness of her cheek, the softness of her hair, and in that moment he forgot that he had once hated her and wished her to suffer. It seemed that they were back together as they once were long ago, Roberto Carvalho was only a shadow, he no longer existed.

"Come in," Nina said, shutting the door behind them.

He sat down in an armchair by the window and he thought how familiar it all seemed, to be once more in a hotel room with Nina. He remembered the Crillon in Paris where they had stayed when Peter was small, and Claridge's in London. They had taken Peter for a ride on one of those red double-decker buses, he could still see the excitement in his eyes watching the boats on the Thames. They were happy then. Those were the bonds he and Nina shared, stronger than she could ever have anyone else. What did it matter that she had married another man? She had not had children with Carvalho. Only with him. That was the one thing that had consoled him during these long years apart, when he had never completely abandoned the hope that Nina would come back to him.

And now she was back again with him, they would console each other in this terrible tragedy, somehow they would find out together where it was that they lost the way.

No man ever loved you the way I did, Nina, he thought, looking at her across the room. No one cared more about your happiness than I did, or the happiness of our children.

"Have they found out ... anything more?" Her words came with difficulty.

He shook his head. "No."

"Who could have done this awful thing?" She kept twisting the rings on her finger and her face in the shadowed room was that of a lost, bewildered child. "Oh why, Lathrop, why? All the way here on the plane I've been asking myself that."

"There are no answers to some things."

"Peter wasn't a person who ... I mean he never got into fights, he hated violence. . . ."

"I know."

"He was always such a quiet little boy. Do you remember that stamp collection he had? He used to spend hours sorting different stamps, pasting them in his book. I wonder whatever happened to that book?"

That was after you left me, Nina. "I don't know," he said. Lost. Lost along with the other things of childhood, the stuffed teddy bear, the tin soldiers, the treasured rock collection. All gone.

"My poor baby. He was always so frightened of thunderstorms. . . ."

Silence, the silence of memories, louder than any thunder. A train going backwards into the yesterday beyond recall.

"I'd better call Ruth Ellen," he said finally.

Nina's eyes narrowed. "What's she like?"

"Unsophisticated. Pretty in a small-town kind of way. Not the kind you'd have expected Peter to choose."

"Then why did he? If he hadn't married her, he might still be alive. If he hadn't stayed out here in this godforsaken place. . . ."

"It was his choice."

"She trapped him into it."

"We don't know that, Nina. She loved him very much. And she's having his child."

"That's just what I mean. She got pregnant and Peter was too honorable to refuse to marry her."

"You're jumping to conclusions."

"No, I don't think so."

"You're not being fair to her, Nina. She's very sweet."

"She's apparently fooled you too."

"Wait till you meet her, you'll see what I mean." Lathrop went over and picked up the telephone. There was something familiar about this scene. Yes, his mother had acted the same way when he told her he wanted to marry Nina. Ironic. He gave the hotel operator the number. He heard it ringing and then Ruth Ellen answered. "Hello, Ruth Ellen," Lathrop said. "This is . . . Dad."

He noticed Nina's look of surprise.

"Yes, I got your message . . . I see. . . . Yes, I'll be right over. Peter's mother has just arrived and we'll be there in a few minutes. . . . Goodbye, my dear."

"What is it?" Nina asked.

"They think they've found a clue. Shall we go?"

"I have to make a phone call first. I promised Roberto I'd call as soon as I got in."

"Can't you send a cable? God knows how long it will take to get a call through."

"If there's a delay I'll try again later. I just want to let Roberto know I've arrived safely so he won't worry."

That bastard Brazilian probably isn't worried anyway, Lathrop thought, sudden bile rising in his throat. "Go ahead, make your call," he said. "I'll take a quick shower and be back in twenty minutes."

❖

He's still jealous of Roberto after all these years, Nina thought, watching Lathrop turn and walk out the door. Poor Lathrop. It all seemed so long ago, unreal now, that marriage they had once shared. Had she ever loved him? she wondered, looking back now to the Nina of seventeen, intent on escape from her dreary life in Baltimore. How many women entered into these youthful marriages and were trapped in them forever, growing old in a kind of barren wilderness, filling the hours with bridge games and endless committees. Were they noble, these women who kept an empty marriage together? And was she selfish and self-centered and all the other names that Lathrop in his anger had called her?

If only Roberto were with her now, she thought, as the operator placed the call to Rio, but of course that would be impossible with Lathrop here. Lathrop was like a stranger to her now, yet he, not Roberto, was the one who had the right to be here. Peter was Lathrop's son, his flesh and blood. The bitter truth is, she thought, that when you have children by a man you are never free of him. You cannot just close the door and say goodbye.

Dimly she had realized this when she asked Lathrop for a divorce, but she had thought that the future would resolve itself. She was in love with Roberto and nothing else mattered but being with him. If only Roberto had cared for her children.

He could have no idea of what she was suffering now.

What was the time difference between Midland and Rio? She could not think clearly, everything was all twisted and turned around. The operator's harsh Texas twang grated on her nerves. She hoped there wouldn't be a delay, she wanted to talk to Roberto now, before Lathrop returned.

She rubbed the back of her neck. It had been hurting ever since she got off the plane. She must have twisted it some way or slept in a draft.

What was taking so long? Perhaps she should have sent a cable after all, but she wanted to hear Roberto's voice, to hear him say that he loved her and was thinking of her.

Night. Yes, it would be night now in Rio.

There seemed to be some confusion. The operator was speaking to someone. The party was not at home. Did Senhora Carvalho wish to speak to anyone else?

Roberto not home? Where could he be? She would ask Maria if he had left some message.

"I'll speak to the person on the line," Nina said.

It was Maria. No, she did not know where the senhor was, he had been gone all evening and had not yet returned. Maria's voice sounded sleepy.

"You're sure Senhor Carvalho did not say where he could be reached?"

Maria was sure.

But where could he be? Nina tried to keep the desperation out of her voice. She was sure the hotel operator was listening. Thank heavens she couldn't understand Portuguese.

"Will you please tell Senhor Carvalho that I have arrived safely and that I will call him later?" she said to Maria.

Nina hung up the phone and started to unpack her suitcase. If Roberto had gone to the Jockey Club or the Gavea Golf Club he could have left the number with Maria, knowing that she would be trying to reach him. And the same thing if he was at the home of one of their friends. She shook the tissue out of the folds of a dress and hung it in the closet. Surely Roberto would have an explanation, but how could he be so inconsiderate? She took her cosmetic kit and started for the bathroom when the telephone rang.

"Hello?"

"Are you ready?" It was Lathrop.

"Just a few more minutes."

"Did you get your call through?"

"Yes." She had no intention of telling Lathrop that she had not found Roberto home. "I just want to change my dress. I'll meet you in the lobby."

"Don't be long. Ruth Ellen is waiting for us."

She felt a sudden pain in the back of her neck again, it seemed to start someplace below her left shoulder blade and travel upwards.

"I'll hurry," she said.

The real and the unreal. Where does one end and the other begin?

Valerie lay on the bed and opened her script. Twenty new pages of dialogue to memorize before tomorrow.

I did love you, Peter, really I did.

Not enough, not enough.

Why did you have to go to Texas? Why?

No, that's the wrong dialogue. Concentrate.

They say you never forget anything. Everything that had happened to you is recorded in your brain, stored away, like the things that were locked in the cellar of their house on Massachusetts Avenue, things that no one wanted anymore, yet could not bear to throw away. The dollhouse with real electric lights that Santa had brought her one Christmas, old valentines, her mother's wedding gown, baby clothes that she and Adele had worn, clay pots and doorstops made at school with childish hands. . . .

She turned a page.

"Keep me safe," she had once said to Peter. He had not understood.

How could she explain the feeling of panic that swept over her so often, of dark wings fluttering, of something waiting to seize her in the shadows? She was lucky, people envied her, they thought of her as confident and secure.

Pictures returned to her, the small protected girl in a blue velvet coat with an ermine hat and muff listening to her father's speeches from the Senate gallery with her mother and Adele. Birthday parties, with her friends coming for showings of Felix the Cat and Mickey Mouse cartoons and ice cream shaped in molds. Playing musical chairs, trying not to be left without a chair when the music stopped. . . .

She had not known Peter then. She had to grow up first, the world would be plunged into war, and then he would find her, like that song of Noel Coward's that she used to play on the victrola. It had been a favorite of her mother's.

Someday I'll find you, moonlight behind you, true to the dream I am dreaming. . . .

The music had stopped. Don't be left without a chair when the music stops, Valerie.

There's one behind you. Sit down quickly!

Images like broken glass, snow on frosty window panes, fragments of blossoms and forgotten music, whirling, whirling, there is no chair, only an empty space, wings brush my cheek, the coffin is gray covered with white lilacs. Feathers of dead birds and silver rain. How temporary is everything in this life!

In the beginning love seems so simple. Why can't it remain that way?

"The victim's wife, Ruth Ellen Spaulding, who is expecting a child in August, said she had no idea who could have wanted to kill her husband."

A child in August. Expecting a child in August. How old would hers be now if . . . no, don't think about it.

Would this Texas sheriff try and contact her about her relationship with Peter? Could they ever find out about the abortion?

No, she had used another name, they could never identify her.

She shuddered. She had forgotten, almost.

Now it all returned, everything, the moments with Peter, the things they had said to each other, the promises. . . .

The pages blurred in front of her.

If only I had gone with him, she thought.

Too late.

The music has stopped, Valerie. There is no chair. Only an empty space.

EIGHTEEN

"You folks been to Midland before?" the cab driver asked
"No," Lathrop said.

That was all he needed to turn him into a one-man Chamber of
Commerce. "Fastest growing city in Texas," he said proudly, "and
getting bigger all the time." He turned a corner "We got everything
here." He pointed to a skyscraper. "More of them things goin' up all
the time." They passed a luxurious old home surrounded by office
buildings. "That there's the Petroleum Club where all the oil men go.
And we got a newer club built just last year, Ranchland Hill. Lots of
the young folks belong to that."

Lathrop threw Nina a helpless glance, wishing the man would
shut up. He wondered why cab drivers always felt obligated to carry
on a conversation with their passengers.

The driver looked over his shoulder. "You folks from back
East?"

"Yes."

"I hear tell it gets real cold there in the winter. Now in Midland,
we have pretty much the same climate all year round. A little hotter in
the summer, but there's always a nice breeze at night to cool things off,

and we don't have no mosquitoes. That's because the elevation here is about twenty-seven hundred feet."

Nina was looking straight ahead with a far-off expression.

"There it is," the driver said suddenly. He pointed to a building that stood in a sand bed with not a tree in sight and what appeared to be a golf course laid out on flat, sandy terrain. "That yonder's Ranchland Hill."

That's a country club? Lathrop thought in amazement.

The cab driver chuckled. "I heard a right good one a few weeks ago about Ranchland Hill. It seems this veteran resident—that's what we call anyone who's been here more'n three years—well, anyhow, he was showing Ranchland Hill to a visitor from New York and he says, 'All this club needs is more water and some shade,' and the New Yorker answers, 'Isn't that about all Hell needs?'" The driver laughed uproariously at this joke, and then, noticing the lack of response from his passengers, he repeated the tag line. "Get the point?"

"Yes, very good," Lathrop said.

He thought suddenly of Wynwood with its magnificent old trees and green lawns and cursed the day he had ever sold it. Peter had loved Wynwood, they had wonderful times there together. He should have kept it, but it all seemed too much for him after his mother's death, and a real estate broker came up with a good offer. As soon as he signed the papers he was sorry, but it was too late.

Too late. He gripped the leather armrest of the cab. Everything appeared to be growing brighter, an intense inner light flooded him. He fumbled in his pocket, where were his pills? His head felt light, things were starting to blur, he knew this sign too well, the terrible illumination that preceded the loss of consciousness. He found the pills and quickly swallowed one.

Must see about having the prescription refilled, he reminded himself, he was almost out. Sometimes he could go for several months without having a seizure, other times one would follow another. No cure, just a cross he must live with.

"Are you all right?" Nina asked.

"Fine." Sweat was running down his face. He took out his cigarette case. His hands were still trembling.

"Do you think it's wise to smoke?" Nina said.

"Why not?"

"Do you still smoke several packs a day?"

"When I feel like it."

"You should cut down. It's terrible for your health."

"I didn't realize my health was of any concern to you, Nina."

She made no reply.

I shouldn't have said that, he thought. The sensitive feelings of the rejected, on the defensive, afraid of being hurt again. But how can you act normal with the person who rejected you for someone else?

"Here you are, folks." The driver pulled up in front of a small green stucco house with the half-finished concrete-block wall enclosing it. "Say, ain't this the place where. . . ." He turned around and stared at his passengers, his mouth hanging open.

Lathrop pulled out his wallet. "How much do I owe you?"

"Uh . . . let's see . . . that'll be . . . three-fifty."

"Keep the change." Lathrop handed him a five-dollar bill and helped Nina out of the cab.

Ruth Ellen brushed her hair and tied it back with a blue ribbon. She was putting on lipstick when the doorbell rang. Here they are, she thought, and her hand shook and made her draw an uneven line around the edge of her mouth. She took a tissue and blotted it. There wasn't time to do it over. She put the mirror down on the bed and reached for her blue-flowered robe.

"Now you just stay put. I'll get it." Mrs. Hankins came out of the kitchen where she had been making coffee. "Remember what the doctor said, we mustn't get over tired."

Mrs. Hankins was a practical nurse, and Doc Kelsey had called her.

"I don't need a nurse," she had protested. "I'm not an invalid."

"I don't like the idea of you being there all alone," Doc Kelsey told her.

"But if I need anything I can always call my neighbors."

She was glad now to have Mrs. Hankins here. She was a cheerful, energetic person, and bustled about tidying up the house and keeping reporters away from the door.

"You go right in, folks," Ruth Ellen heard her say. "I'll get you some chairs."

Ruth Ellen looked up as Lathrop and Nina came in the bedroom. So this is Senhora Carvalho, she thought, looking at the chic woman in black beside Peter's father, a woman who was beautiful even in grief, a woman she could not ever imagine calling "Mother." Yes, she could see now where Peter had gotten his looks, they had the same bone structure, the same coloring, though Peter's eyes were more blue and somehow softer.

"Here we are," said Mrs. Hankins. She placed a chair on either side of the bed. "Is there anything I can get you folks? Some coffee?"

"There's some just made," Ruth Ellen said.

"That would be very nice," said Nina. "Thank you." She sat down and glanced around the room, her eyes stopping at a photograph of Peter on the bureau.

"Would it bother you if I smoked?" Lathrop asked.

"No, of course not," Ruth Ellen said.

Nina was still staring at the photograph. "That was taken just before he went overseas," she said.

Mrs. Hankins returned with the coffee. "Cream or sugar?"

"Just black, please," said Lathrop.

"The same for me," Nina said.

Like statues sitting there stiffly, Ruth Ellen thought, those two who were responsible for Peter's life, parents, now strangers, as much to each other as to her, yet all tied by a common bond, the thread that held them all: Peter.

Each with their separate memories, sitting there in silence.

And she thought how we all leave pieces of ourselves behind in others' lives, and to each person we are different. Who has the complete picture of anyone?

If the fragments were all gathered together . . . but that is not possible, they are scattered too far and too wide, and there are always the missing pieces, the unknown love, the secret vice, the buried dream. All those, and more.

Lathrop put down his coffee. "There are some things I'll need of Peter's," he said, glancing toward the closet. "A suit, a pair of shoes. . . ."

For the undertaker, Ruth Ellen thought. "I think his dark suit is back from the cleaner's," she said. For a party, I sent it to be cleaned for a party, and instead he's being buried in it. Oh, God. . . .

"A shirt?"

She pointed to the bureau.

"I'll drop these off at the funeral home," Lathrop said, gathering up the clothes. ."And then the sheriff wants to see me at the courthouse." Nina started to rise. "There's no point in your coming, Nina. You stay here with Ruth Ellen and I'll be back as soon as I can."

The room was small with white stucco walls, the floor covered with a dirty tan rug. Lathrop looked up into the bright glare from the ceiling light set in soundproofing squares with dots, his palms were sweating as they gripped the arms of the brown leather chair, the rubber bands across his stomach and chest resembled black snake coils. The sergeant wrapped a black rubberish cloth tightly around his upper left arm and handed him a silver metal band attached to a chain.

"Hold this in your left hand," he said.

Directly ahead was a long narrow window with closed venetian blinds. Lathrop turned his head. The sergeant opened the top drawer of a brown metal filing cabinet in the corner and took out a tan manila envelope. He put graph paper in the portable lie detector machine sitting on the desk and adjusted the needles. Lathrop noticed a bell button set in a block of wood next to the machine and a black metal ashtray with gold edges containing a half-smoked cigarette and matches. What he wouldn't give for a cigarette now! Drops of perspiration rolled down his face, his heart was beating more rapidly. Relax, he told himself, you're not on trial. You volunteered to take this test.

The room seemed to be getting smaller, it was closing in on him.

It was like the dream, the same terrible dream recurring again and again with slight variations. He was in a room and suddenly the ceiling caved in on him, he could see cracks appear and dust from the plaster trickling down and then it broke off in hunks, huge pieces were falling on him, he could taste plaster in his mouth and he was struggling for air, the weight was crushing him. One time he was caught in quicksand, and in another dream he was in a tunnel that collapsed. Then there was the dream where he was walking across an open field and the earth started to rumble and without warning the ground split open and he fell in, he was falling, down, down. . . .

He wondered what a psychiatrist would make of his nightmares.

"We'll start in a minute," the sergeant said. "Is that blood pressure band too tight? I can loosen it if you'd like."

There was a small square mirror on the wall in back of the desk. It needed cleaning. Or was it really a mirror? Lathrop suddenly remembered a detective story he had once read. The lie-detector room had another room behind it where the prisoner could be watched through a window while he was taking the test. Was someone watching him now?

Why should they be? He wasn't a prisoner.

The sergeant was staring at him. He had a black bulb in his hand that attached to the blood pressure band. "Just tell me when it feels comfortable, Mr. Spaulding."

"That's better now," Lathrop said. His throat felt dry and constricted. Who could feel comfortable strapped in this contraption? It was like an electric chair with the warden waiting to pull the switch. Does the prisoner have a last request?

"All right? Now remember, try to relax and we'll get better results. Look directly ahead of you and imagine you're in your living room having a conversation with a friend."

Very funny. Texas joke. Out of the corner of his eye Lathrop saw the sergeant adjust the machine and start it. He had a paper beside him.

"Is your real name Lathrop Spaulding?"

Of course. What else would it be? Lathrop felt anger rising in him, he turned and looked at the sergeant.

"Just answer yes or no."

"Yes." Must stay calm. They started with general questions, the same for everyone. Some people didn't give their real names when booked, that's why they asked that question.

"Do you drive a white Cadillac convertible?"

"Yes." Lathrop could see the three needles making red wavy lines on the graph paper in the machine.

"Please look straight ahead and not at the machine. You couldn't read it anyway," the sergeant said. "Do you have any idea who would have wanted to murder your son?" His voice still had the same conversational drawl, as if he were asking the time of day.

Lathrop started, and the black coils pressed tighter. "No, I haven't."

"Did you ever hear your son speak of Dave Creighton?"

"Yes. He shared an apartment with him." The metal band felt cold and clammy across his wet palm.

"Did your son have any friends who were homosexuals?"

"No." Lathrop could feel his blood pressure rising. What was the name of that boy Peter used to see a lot of in Washington, the one with the limp lock of hair always hanging over his face? He had a way of waving his hands in the air when he spoke, he looked like a damned fairy and some people thought he was, but Peter said it wasn't true, that he just had unfortunate mannerisms. Suddenly, without any explanation, Peter stopped seeing him. He must have been about fifteen then. These bastards checked on everything. Guilt by association. "No," he repeated, more vehemently than he intended. "My son hated queers."

Out of the corner of his eye Lathrop saw the sergeant write something on a slip of paper. Why had he agreed to take this test in the first place? What were they trying to prove? That Peter had homosexual tendencies? Well that was a damned lie. Peter had always gone for girls and let them try and find evidence to the contrary.

"Did anyone in your family suffer from mental illness?"

"No. Not that I know of." His head was throbbing now. There were rumors about his father's death, things that were never fully explained, but he had not questioned them, perhaps because he was afraid of what he would find out. And his own ailment was not a mental illness, though there were still ignorant people who thought so. The blood pressure band on his arm felt tight again. He shifted uncomfortably in the chair.

"Would you say that you had a close relationship with your son?"

"Yes."

"He discussed his activities with you?"

"Sometimes." When he was smaller, yes, it was a long time ago, he spoke of the things they did at school, they talked about sports, his interest in flying, he used to help Peter build model planes. Then it all changed.

"Did he ask your advice about business?"

"No."

"He didn't consult you about going to Midland?"

"No." Peter had just taken off. He had gotten a letter from him saying he was going to go into the oil business. It was all very sudden. He had a job for a while in the reservation department of Capital Airlines after he got out of the service, but he felt there was no future for him in that. He should have gone back and finished college. He'd told him that. "If you don't want to go back to Princeton, go somewhere else, but finish your education." Peter hadn't listened. He was restless after the war, drifting like a ship without a harbor, like so many young men of his generation. The generation they called lost, but what generation could say they had found the answers? Fathers spoke and sons did what they wanted, looked for their own paths. Experience cannot be passed on.

"That's all, Mr. Spaulding." The sergeant stood up and unwound the arm band and unstrapped the coils. Lathrop noticed the revolver in the holster attached to his belt, and handcuffs and keys. "Right through that door," he said, pointing. "The sheriff would like to see you again."

NINETEEN

T he telephone rang in Lathrop's hotel room. He reached over and picked it up.

"It's Jake Birney," said the voice. "Can you talk? I'm in the lobby."

About time he heard from that private investigator, he thought. He was beginning to wonder if he'd skipped town or something. "Yes, I'm alone. Come on up."

He poured himself a strong bourbon and then added a little water. He wanted to be sober to hear what Birney had to say. Afterwards was another thing. Somehow he had the uneasy feeling that he would rather not know what was coming. He stood looking out the window at a neon sign flashing above a gas station and then he heard a rap on the door.

Jake Birney was of medium height and build with receding black hair and an acne-scarred complexion. He wore heavy horn-rimmed glasses and carried a large manila envelope.

"Would you like a drink?" Lathrop asked.

"Thanks. I never drink on the job."

"Did you find out who did it?"

"I'm working on it. I've got some pretty good leads—"

"Is that all you wanted to tell me?" Lathrop's face flushed. "At a hundred dollars a day plus expenses—"

"Now take it easy, Mr. Spaulding. This isn't going to be an easy case to crack. And it's only been a couple days since—"

"I know how long it's been since my son was murdered." He grabbed Birney by the coat lapels. "I want his killer brought to justice!"

"Like I said, it's not easy. I think I'll change my mind about the drink, if you don't mind."

"I'm drinking bourbon."

"Bourbon's fine with me."

Lathrop poured Birney a drink and waited. There was something shifty and underhanded about this man used to dealing with the most sordid aspects of human behavior. He wondered what would make a man become a private detective.

Birney took a sip of his drink. "Good bourbon. Now, we've got to come up with a motive. Someone wanted your son out of the way and for a good reason." He looked at Lathrop. "You can't think of anyone who might have that reason?"

Lathrop shook his head. There were so many things about Peter that he didn't know. Other than the fellow he'd shared an apartment with when he first came to Midland, he'd never heard Peter speak of any of his friends here. Or enemies.

"Your son served in Italy during the war. Did he keep in contact with any of his army buddies?"

"Not that I'm aware of." But how would he be?

"Because sometimes people from the past crop up and expect a debt repaid, and then. . . ."

"Just what are you getting at?"

"Well, you know, Italy, the Cosa Nostra. Your son could have gotten in with some people when he was in Italy at the end of the war—"

"My son served with distinction during the war. He was awarded the silver star personally by General Mark Clark. He was an officer and a gentleman."

"Yeah, but—" Birney shrugged.

"Are you implying that my son got involved with the Mafia and they put out a contract on him?"

"Stranger things have happened. I'm just trying to cover all bases. The information you've given me so far hasn't been too helpful."

"I don't know what else to tell you. It's up to you to find out the facts."

"Well for that I'll need a little more money. I may have to grease a few palms to get people to talk."

"How much?"

"Five hundred should do."

Lathrop took out his checkbook.

"Cash."

"Then I'll have to go down to the desk and cash some traveler's checks. I don't have that much cash on me."

"Fine. I'll go with you."

"If you don't mind waiting in the hall, I'll be right back with the money." Lathrop locked his room and pocketed the key.

"Oh, sure. I understand."

Lathrop felt the private investigator's eyes following him as he walked to the elevator.

Billie was nude except for high boots, a diamond necklace, and a cowboy hat. In one hand she held a long whip. Tied to a chair was Earl Copeland, also nude. Across his back were several red welts.

"Okay, that's enough, baby," he said. "You can untie me now."

She knelt down beside him, her breasts brushing his arm, and loosened the rope, wondering when he would tire of this game. In her time she'd had some kinky sex, but Earl was something else. Well, if it made him happy. . . .

He stood up and put his arms around her. "Now kiss it and make it well," he said.

She heard her neighbors in the next apartment turning the key in their door and wondered how much they could hear through the walls.

"You're a great gal, Billie. I don't know what I'd do without you."

"You'd manage."

"I'd have married you long ago if it hadn't been for—"

"I know. At least that's what you're always telling me."

"What the hell am I supposed to do? It don't look right for a man to divorce an invalid wife. I had no idea she'd hang on this long. There's been nothing between Jo Beth and me for years You know that."

"Yes, Earl, I know."

"Stick with me, baby. You'll be the governor's wife yet."

She sat up in bed. "I didn't know you planned to run for governor."

"Yeah, in the next election."

"And what about Jo Beth?"

"What about her? She's my wife as long as she lives. But I don't think that's going to be too much longer."

Billie rolled over on her back.

"You keep all this under your hat, y'hear? I know I don't have to say that, because I've always known I could trust you."

"Of course, Earl."

He grabbed her suddenly by the hair. "I can trust you, can't I, Billie?"

"Earl, you're hurting me."

"Then answer me!"

"Yes, Earl, you can trust me."

"Because if I ever thought I couldn't. . . ."

He let go of her hair and, without any preliminaries, he straddled her and thrust himself into her.

TWENTY

*I*t had to happen to a guy like Peter, it was inevitable, thought Dave Creighton. Sooner or later things were bound to catch up with him. You can't play around with dynamite and not have it go off. That's why he'd gotten away, he didn't want to be around to see the explosion.

He wasn't surprised when the sheriff called him from Midland. The only surprise was that they could think he had a reason for wanting Peter killed. Sure, he was bitter about losing an eye. Who wouldn't be? But things were going pretty good for him now in Denver and he didn't want to go back to Midland for any inquest.

He adjusted the black patch over his left eye. He'd never had much luck with girls before, but this made him kind of a romantic figure. He'd changed the story of how it really happened. No sense telling them he was shot through a window by mistake when they were after his buddy. His version was much more colorful and made him seem like the hero of one of those Jack London books. He didn't want the real story coming out in the newspapers.

Besides, he'd told the sheriff all he knew right after it happened. Well, almost. They were supposed to be protecting Peter. Great protection!

Yes, he'd been smart to pull out of Midland when he did. He'd seen some pretty rough characters in his twenty-nine years, but none to compare with those oil sharks. Peter was no match for them.

He scratched his head.

He wouldn't put it past that redhead to have been involved in the whole mess. What was her name? Billie . . . yeah, that was it. When you fool around with another man's dame you're just asking for it, and he'd told Peter so.

I guess when you come from a background like Peter's you think you can get away with anything, he thought. Oh, sure he'd envied him. The guy had things handed to him on a silver platter. Good looks, money, society family, girls falling for him right and left, he didn't have to lift a finger, just looked at them in that quiet way of his and they tumbled. Funny thing was, none of it seemed to make him happy. Come to think of it, he was the unhappiest guy he'd ever known.

How do you figure that?

Sure, he'd envied him, but he didn't now. He was alive and Peter was dead.

He wasn't someone you could get close to, he thought, looking back. Kinda clammed up when you got on anything personal. They'd shared an apartment for nearly six months and he couldn't say he really knew him.

Most guys he'd known did a lot of bragging, especially about the war. You'd think they'd all won it single-handed. He admitted he'd done his share about his hitch in the Navy as a seaman on a minesweeper, but Peter was a real hero, had the French Croix de Guerre or whatever that medal was and never mentioned it.

He remembered once when they were talking about Germans he'd said to Peter, "The only good Krauts are the dead ones."

"No, that's not true," Peter said. "When I was a boy I had a German nurse. She was a wonderful woman. She used to tell me fairy stories about the Black Forest and I loved her very much. More than. . . ." He had not finished the sentence, and Dave wondered whether he was going to say that he loved his nurse more than his own mother, and then they had gotten off on another subject and Peter never mentioned it again.

Peter wasn't a guy you could sit around and talk about dames with either. He acted as if you were invading private territory or something. He had a picture of a blonde on his bureau and there were letters that came in scented blue envelopes with fancy handwriting. He'd made some kind of crack to Peter like, "That's a pretty classy-looking broad. Is she any good in the hay?"

Peter looked furious. "She's not a broad," he said, and walked out of the apartment.

Not long afterwards he put the picture away and the blue envelopes stopped.

A strange guy. Well, everyone had some odd quirks.

He wondered what would have happened if Peter hadn't gone to the movies that night, but they got him in the end, so it worked out the same way.

Poor Peter. Dave shook his head. He was damned sorry about the whole thing, he really was.

❖

The Spaulding file was growing thicker and still no results. The longer this case dragged on the less chance of solving it, and danged if he was going to have another unsolved murder on his record, Sheriff Mahoney thought.

He went through the file again. There wasn't enough evidence to hold anyone. Everyone had an alibi. All they could hope for was that someone would talk. If only one person was involved the chances of finding him were slim, but if there was a plot and several people knew about it. . . .

Yes, that must be the answer. Eventually someone would squeal and then they could make an arrest. Meanwhile it was a matter of sifting through everything over and over again, and checking anyone who had any connection, no matter how slight, with young Spaulding.

Suddenly he had an idea. He buzzed for the deputy.

"I'd like to question that bellboy at the Scharbauer Hotel," he said. "The Mexican."

❖

"Your name?" the sheriff asked.

"Manuel López."

"Age?"

"Twenty-two."

"How long have you worked at the Scharbauer Hotel?"

"About eight . . . no, ten months."

"As bellboy?"

He shifted uncomfortably. "Sometimes I do other jobs."

"Such as?"

"I get whiskey and . . ."

"Drugs?"

"No." He looked frightened. "No drugs."

"Women?"

He looked at the floor.

"You'd better speak up, boy."

"Sometimes . . . the men . . . they ask me do I know any girls."

"That's better. You tell the truth and you'll be all right. We know your sister's a prostitute."

Manuel looked at the sheriff with hatred.

"And she has friends. Right?"

"Sí."

"You get a cut from what her customers pay?"

Manuel squirmed in his chair.

"Answer me, you greasy Mexican!"

"I do not know what it is you want from me."

"Well don't you worry your head none about that. How come you came to Midland from . . ." Sheriff Mahoney glanced at a paper on his desk,"Abajo." He mispronounced the name. "New Mexico's a far piece from here."

"You ever been in Abajo, *señor*?"

"Can't say as I have."

Manuel looked out the window. "It is near Albuquerque. A village. We were eight children. No father. We live in a clay house with broken windows next to the railroad tracks. Dust everywhere, the trees, they are thirsty for water. No rain in Abajo. We play in the dirt. The big thing is when the Super Chief go by. I see people looking out the train, I want to get on it, to go anywhere, just to get away from Abajo. You understand?"

Sheriff Mahoney understood but he did not say so. "How did you get to Midland?"

"I walk to Albuquerque. At the railroad station there are old Indian women selling rugs, turquoise bracelets. The people get off the train and buy. I see that the ones from Texas have many pesetas to spend. I talk to them."

"Your English is pretty good. Where did you learn it?"

Manuel shrugged. "I go to school in Abajo several years. The rest I pick up here and there."

"You worked in Albuquerque?"

"At gas station. Texaco."

"And how did you get here?"

"I service car for man. He has fine boots, expensive. I admire. I tell him I want to go to Texas. He gives me ride."

"Just like that?"

"I do not know what you mean, *señor*."

"He didn't want something in return?"

"He said perhaps he could find job for me."

"Did he get you your job at the Scharbauer?"

"*Sí.*"

"Do you know what he does?"

"He is oil man." Manuel grinned. "Big oil man. Lotsa money."

"Can you give me his name?"

"Señor Copeland."

"You do jobs for him on the side?"

"Sometimes when he has friends I find girls. He likes young ones. He tell me his wife is *enferma* . . . sick . . . for long time."

"Did you ever hear him speak of Peter Spaulding?"

"No. I know nothing. *Nada.*"

"I thought perhaps you might hear something and if you did. . . ."

"This is reason why you sent for me? I know nothing, *señor.*"

"There is a reward for any information leading to the arrest of Peter Spaulding's killer. You understand?" Sheriff Mahoney saw a gleam come into the boy's eyes and he knew that he had judged him correctly. "We'd be much obliged if you would tell us anything you find out."

Manuel looked scared.

"Don't worry. We'll protect you."

"I do what I can. I can go now?"

"Yes." Sheriff Mahoney stood up. "*Adiós,* Manuel." He held out his hand.

Manuel looked at the hand but did not shake it. "*Adiós,*" he said.

Sheriff Mahoney did not see his look of contempt.

TWENTY-ONE

Nina took out her key.

"You're sure you can sleep?" Lathrop asked.

"Yes. Anyway, I have some pills in my bag."

"If you need anything, I'm right down the hall." He kissed her on the cheek. "Call me when you wake up."

Nina closed the door and leaned wearily against it. Still no call from Roberto. Had Maria given him her message? She walked over to the phone and picked up the receiver. "I'd like to place a call to Rio de Janeiro," she said, and gave the operator the number.

She lay on the bed and kicked off her shoes, still holding the phone.

"What? It's in Brazil. South America." God, these Texans! She felt as if she were holding herself together with a piece of thread that might snap at any minute. The whole day had been too much for her. Everything. Roberto, where are you? I want you with me now, I need to hear your voice, I don't think I can stand any more.

It had been a strain seeing Lathrop again after all this time, like opening the door to a dark closet she had locked long ago, stored with things she never wanted to see again.

"Yes? . . . All right, call me back when you get the party on the line."

Her head was throbbing with a dull headache from all the medication Doctor Silva had given her. She went into the bathroom and swallowed two aspirins. Where had Roberto been all evening? The thought tortured her. Visions of Roberto with another woman went through her mind, Roberto laughing and happy while she was suffering. She switched off the bedroom light and lay in the dark, her head pressed against the pillow. She heard water dripping, it was coming from the tap, she had not turned it off completely. Splash, splash, like a metronome it continued, water splashing, it could be a lovely sound if it was a fountain, like the sound of the fountain in the courtyard of their hotel in Paris, the Paris of her honeymoon with Roberto. . . .

❖

The courtyard of the Plaza-Athénée had red umbrellas and on each table was a hurricane lamp with a red candle in frosted gold glass and a bouquet of mixed summer flowers in a silver vase. Nina unfolded a napkin printed with red poppies and smiled at Roberto.

"I'm glad you chose this hotel, darling," she said.

"It is my favorite in Paris. I hoped you would like it. I only wish I could show you Paris for the first time, that you had never been here before."

"I have never been here before. Not really."

At the next table an elderly couple, the only other people in the dining room, were looking at a menu.

"Why don't they print it in English?" the woman complained. Her plumpness was not enhanced by her wildly-figured silk dress and she had a flat Midwestern accent.

The husband snapped his fingers at a waiter. "You'll have to translate this for me," he said. "I can't read French."

The waiter went over and got the captain.

"May I assist you, sir?"

"Yes. What does all this stuff mean?"

Nina caught a flicker of amusement in Roberto's eye as the captain started to translate a menu with a polite but somewhat disdainful manner. It was Bastille Day and most of the restaurants were closed. In fact, most of the Parisians left Paris in July and Roberto's friends were all in Cap Ferrat or some vacation spot along the Riviera, so there was no one they had to see and they could be alone. She was glad after their weeks of parties in London, where Roberto was always running into people he knew.

"We'll drive out into the country tomorrow," Roberto said. "I know a charming little inn where we can have luncheon. A village called Barbizon."

"*Les Escargots Bourguignonne* . . . what's that?" the woman at the next table asked in an atrocious attempt at French.

"Snails, Madame," the captain said. "With a sauce—"

"Ugh," she said, making a face.

"Got a good steak?" the husband asked.

The captain lifted one eyebrow. "May I suggest *Le Filet de Boeuf Wellington?*"

"What's that?"

"It is filet of beef baked in puff pastry with truffle sauce."

"I like everything plain."

"Oh, Ralph, let's try it. It sounds good."

"It's not going to agree with your gall bladder, Mother," he told his wife. "You'll be sorry tonight."

"I'm going to have it anyway. I can't get filet of beef whatever it is in Cedar Rapids."

"I hope they're not staying at this hotel," Roberto whispered.

Nina laughed. "They probably have the next room."

The couple was staring at them.

"Where are you folks from?" the man asked.

"I am so sorry," Roberto said in his most charming manner. "I do not speak the English."

"See, Ralph, I told you they were French."

"Well I'm just trying to be friendly," the man said. "They can all speak English if they want to."

"You know what I'd like to do when we finish dinner?" Nina said.

"What is that?"

"I'd like to watch the fireworks from the Pont Neuf."

"Oh. I was hoping you had something else in mind."

Nina smiled. "That too. Later."

"The fireworks are really only for the tourists."

"Well, I'm a tourist then. After all, how often is one in Paris on Bastille Day?"

"If that would give you pleasure, *querida*, that is what we shall do."

They watched the fireworks exploding in the skies above the Tuileries and the Louvre, little dreaming that in a few years Paris would be in darkness, echoing to the sounds of German boots and the rumble of artillery, with swastikas hanging from the buildings and Nazi officers occupying their hotel. But tonight Paris was theirs, city of lights and gaiety and lovers.

Later, lying in Roberto's arms, hearing the water splashing in the courtyard fountain, she thought that she had never known such happiness. She had completely forgotten Peter, Marcia, any other life, nothing else existed but this.

Had she been selfish wanting beauty and romance, the unforgettable moments of love with Roberto, so different from what she had known with Lathrop? Lathrop's lovemaking was crude and animal-like, after which he fell immediately into a heavy sleep, leaving her restless and unsatisfied, staring into the dark, and wondering if there wasn't more to love than that.

Lathrop accused her of being frigid, and one night in his anguish he said, "Maybe you'd be different with another man." He had read her thoughts. She knew she was only waiting for someone else, and when she saw Roberto that time at Virginia Beach, she knew who the man was.

It was almost a year before their paths crossed again, and then she knew it was fate. She was visiting friends in Washington and went with them to a garden party at the British Embassy. Roberto Carvalho was there. She saw him across the crowded lawn, watching her with an amused look.

"Mrs. Spaulding and I have met before," he said when they were introduced. "How nice to see you again."

It had not occurred to her to move to Washington before that. She only knew that she was going to leave Lathrop, but where she was going after that she had no idea. Fate had stepped in now and she would follow where he led, for fate had one name only and that was Roberto.

The phone was ringing by her bed.

"I have your party now, ma'am."

"Thank you." She waited. "Roberto?"

"*Querida*, I have been so anxious about you. I went out for just a short time and Maria said you had telephoned. I was just trying to reach you."

"Oh, my darling, it's so good to hear your voice!" What did it matter if he was lying? She loved him, she would always love him, no matter what he did. "It's so awful here, I wish you were with me."

"I have been thinking of you constantly, *querida*. I know how terrible this is for you."

There was a crackling sound on the line. "I can't hear you very well," she said.

"It is a poor connection. Is there anything I can do for you here?"

"No. I'll send you a cable when I know what flight I'm taking back."

"I wish I could help you, my darling."

"It helps just talking to you."

"Just know that I am with you."

"I know. Goodnight, my dearest. I love you," she said.

❖

Lathrop undressed and got into bed but he could not sleep. Nina, he thought. It was still Nina, would always be Nina. He wondered if she was lying awake too and if she would like a nightcap. He started to pick up the phone and then put it down. No. He saw the taunting look in her eyes, the look that had hurt him so many times.

Why did she still have a hold on him after all these years?

He knew many beautiful women. Men grew spoiled in New York, especially if they had money and an attractive bachelor apartment. Women were constantly calling with invitations to dinner parties, the theatre, a weekend on Long Island or in Bucks County. They all tired him. He liked to do his own chasing.

The rich women drank too much and used foul language. The models didn't drink, they were too worried about their looks, but they were grasping for money and always wanted to be seen at El Morocco or "21."

And then there was Nina. But Nina was gone, she was lost to him forever.

A thought occurred to him. Perhaps . . . no, there was no point in hoping, he had gone through all that before. But with Nina back, life would have some meaning. How long could she stay with that bastard Carvalho? He had pointed out his faults to her but that only made her defend him. Wrong strategy. There was nothing more futile than trying to convince a woman that she was in love with a heel. She would have to discover it herself.

He got up and took a strong sleeping pill.

He dreamt he was going up a steep, steep hill in the old family Packard with the chauffeur and his mother. The hill went straight up and he could not see the top, he was terrified that the car would roll backward. He started to shake and then a sound woke him. He could sense someone in his room. Slowly, he opened his eyes. In the dark he thought he could make out a figure standing by the bureau.

"Who is it? What do you want?" he said.

The figure turned and slipped out the door without answering. Lathrop turned on the light and looked at his watch. Three o'clock.

A drawer was half open and the contents dumped on the floor. His wallet was still there but it was empty. He looked for his gold Dunhill lighter. Nina had given it to him one Christmas. It was gone.

He picked up the phone and rang the desk.

"This is Mr. Spaulding in three fifty-two," he said. "I've just been robbed. . . Yes, that's what I said. Someone was in my room. . . Well by God, you'd better do something about it before morning! Send up the manager and the house detective right away!" He slammed down the phone.

He felt groggy, his tongue was thick, and there was a bitter taste in his mouth.

He went into the bathroom and splashed cold water on his face. It didn't help.

There was a knock on the door.

"Yes?" Lathrop said.

"Assistant manager. Did you want me?"

Lathrop opened the door. "I asked for the manager."

"Mr. Mitchell isn't available," he said, glancing around the room and then back at Lathrop with a look used to placating angry guests. "I understand there's been a little trouble?"

"You might call it that. Someone came in my room while I was asleep and robbed me."

"Did you have the chain on your door?"

"I don't remember. The door was locked."

"We always ask our guests to put on the night chain. Just a precautionary measure."

"Does this sort of thing happen often?"

"Oh no," he said quickly. "Now, what is missing?"

"A hundred and fifty dollars in cash and a gold lighter."

"We always suggest that our guests put any valuables in the hotel safe," he said with an oily smile, and Lathrop felt a sudden desire to punch him in the nose. "However, I'll make a report on it. I'm very sorry this happened, Mr. Spaulding."

"I'd like to see the manager in the morning," Lathrop said.

"Mr. Mitchell will be in his office at nine," the assistant said. He made a hasty exit.

Lathrop got back into bed. He was now completely awake and he didn't want to take another sleeping pill. If only he had gotten a better look at the person who was in his room, but it had been too dark and he just caught a fleeting glimpse of him. It was a man, that much he had seen, but he would never be able to identify him.

And had the robber just picked his room by accident or was it deliberate?

He must have had a key to unlock the door.

The assistant manager's attitude infuriated him the more he thought about it. What were you supposed to do, sleep with a gun under your pillow?

He stared into the darkness and he felt a sharp, unbearable pain. Peter, he thought, my son. The pain would never go away, it would be with him always.

Dawn came and he was still awake.

TWENTY-TWO

"**W**here did they find him?" Sheriff Mahoney asked.

"In that alley back of Joe's bar. Looks like he put up one hell of a fight. There were broken bottles and overturned garbage pails everywhere, not to mention blood. A real mess," the coroner said. He pulled back the sheet.

The body was in his early twenties, well built, with a swarthy complexion and dark curly hair. His throat was slit and there were multiple stab wounds in his chest.

"Any identification on him?" Sheriff Mahoney asked. He knew who it was.

"His wallet was gone. This is all we found." The coroner handed Sheriff Mahoney a gold cigarette lighter. "Looks too expensive to be his. Probably stole it."

Sheriff Mahoney turned the lighter over and saw the initials L.S. He looked back at the body lying on the slab. The lips seemed to curl downwards in a sneer.

Have you ever been in Abajo, señor? We play in the dirt. The trees there, they are thirsty for water.

You would have been better off in Abajo, Manuel López, he thought.

❖

"Carmen López?"

The pretty young Mexican waitress in the coffee shop of the Scharbauer Hotel looked up from the table she was clearing and smiled, then noticing Sheriff Mahoney's badge, a flicker of fear showed in her eyes. "*Sí?*"

"I'd like to talk to you when you get off work."

She continued stacking the dirty plates onto a tray. "It will not be for an hour, *señor*."

"That's all right. I'll wait."

He sat down at a table in the corner and ordered an enchilada and a beer, then lit a cigar. She probably figures I want to pay for her other services, he thought watching her, and she wouldn't be hard to take. The girl had a Latin lushness, the kind that would fade early the way so many of them did, but now she was like a ripe mango.

He flushed. He must not think such things, he was here for another reason and he had a job to do. First he would have to find out what she knew, then inform her of her brother's death. It was not a task he was looking forward to. In spite of her bright scarlet lipstick and heavy green eye shadow, there was a pathetic look of vulnerability about her.

We were eight children. No father. We live in a clay house next to the railroad tracks.

He heard Manuel's words again. Poor families were close usually, they clung to each other, unlike the rich ones he had observed who were always squabbling over money. She would probably take it hard.

But you can't waste no sympathy in the job he had, he reminded himself. He took a bite of his enchilada. It was good.

❖

Carmen led Sheriff Mahoney up a flight of stairs to her room above a furniture store. A colorful Spanish shawl was tossed over sheets that looked none too clean and on the wall above the bed he noticed a crucifix. There was a bureau that had seen better times and a sink in the corner with a cracked mirror.

Ironic, he thought, that crucifix staring down at the bed where she brought her customers. In his younger days he had once taken out a Catholic girl and they spent Saturday night together. Sunday morning she said she had to get up and go to Mass, and when it was over she was right glad to crawl back in bed with him again and screw some more. A strange religion, Catholicism.

"Please sit down, *señor*," Carmen said, pointing to a red brocade armchair trimmed with torn fringe, the only chair in the room, and then she sat on the edge of the bed and waited, a wary look in her eyes.

"You needn't be afraid, Carmen," the sheriff said. "I just want to ask you a few questions."

She sat watching him, still distrustful.

"How long have you been in Midland?" he asked.

"Three months, *señor*."

"Did your brother suggest you come here?"

"Yes. Manuel, he send me bus fare."

"I see." He paused. "You are close to Manuel?"

She smiled. "Ah, yes, Manuel, he my favorite brother. He very good to me and mama and the little ones."

"Did Manuel ever mention Peter Spaulding to you?"

"Mention? I do not understand."

"Did Manuel say anything to you about him?"

"The man who was killed?" She shook her head. "No, *señor*."

"There is a reward for any information leading to the arrest of Peter Spaulding's killer," he said, not taking his eyes from her face.

How many days ago had he spoken those very same words to Manuel? And now he was dead, also violently.

"I know nothing. I wish I could help you, *señor*, but I cannot."

The girl appeared to be telling the truth or else she was a very skillful liar, he thought. "What do you know about Earl Copeland?"

She shrugged. "I have met him."

"More than once?"

"Several times. I did not like him."

"Why not?"

"It is a feeling I get, I do not know why."

"Was he a customer of yours?" He indicated the bed. "Did Earl Copeland come here?"

"No, never."

"But he sent friends to you?"

She looked at the floor and said nothing.

She'd better not play coy with me, he thought. "He arranged for you to entertain his friends?" he said.

"Sometimes."

"And he got Manuel his job at the hotel, didn't he?"

"Yes."

"Tell me, Carmen, when did you last see your brother?" He tossed it off casually but she was immediately apprehensive and he noticed her body stiffen.

"Manuel is in some kind of trouble?" she asked nervously.

"When did you last see him?" he repeated.

She thought a minute. "Two days ago."

He chose his words carefully. "Do you know of anyone who would have wanted to harm him?"

"Something has happened to Manuel?" She clasped her hands over her breasts. "That is what you have come to tell me?"

"Yes, I'm afraid so. I'm sorry."

"Manuel is dead?"

Sheriff Mahoney nodded. "His body was found in an alley. He had been stabbed many times."

"*Madre de Dios!*" She let out an animal scream, her eyes wild, and crumpled over on the bed. He sat watching her cry and when she finally raised her head, tears had streaked her face with black mascara. "Where is he now?" she asked in a hoarse whisper.

"The body is at the morgue," he said. "Come, Carmen, I'll take you there. We need a positive identification from a family member."

TWENTY-THREE

Ruth Ellen awoke. Today was Peter's funeral. She shivered, wondering how she was going to get through it without collapsing hysterically and making a spectacle of herself. In the closet a black maternity dress hung like a shroud, waiting for her to get up and put it on. It once had a pink linen collar, but she had ripped that off. She never wore hats so she had borrowed a black pillbox with a veil from her neighbor.

Tornado was lying on the foot of the bed watching her with mournful brown eyes. She reached over and patted him and he licked her hand. Impulsively she hugged him and burst into tears.

Mrs. Hankins came in with her breakfast tray.

"I'm not hungry," Ruth Ellen told her. "I'll just have coffee."

"You'll do no such thing," Mrs. Hankins said. "Now you eat something or you'll faint in church."

Ruth Ellen drank the orange juice and pushed the scrambled eggs around the plate with her fork.

Mrs. Hankins crossed her arms over her chest. "I'm going to stand right here till you finish."

She felt dizzy and nauseated, but Mrs. Hankins was right, she must force herself to eat.

I am a widow, she thought, and the word seemed alien to her. She associated it with old age, with lonely old women eating dinner alone, working at church bazaars. But I am still young, I will have my baby to care for and I will not be alone.

It was hard to think of the future, it stretched before her like an endless road with no signposts, only a blank highway leading nowhere.

She would not stay in Midland, that she knew, she could not bear this house without Peter, with the constant reminder of everything that had happened. She had to get away.

Flowers were arriving and Mrs. Hankins was opening the cards and writing names on a list.

As soon as the baby was born and able to travel they would move to Houston. She had a girlfriend there, and when the baby was older she could get a job. Mr. Garrison would give her a good recommendation.

Keep going, she told herself, you've got to. You can't just give up. She knew that no man would ever exist for her again, she was resigned to that. Like my mother, she thought suddenly.

Mrs. Hankins picked up a spray of yellow roses. "My, these sure are pretty," she said, sniffing them. "Do you want these to go to the church?"

Ruth Ellen opened the card. On it was written simply: Valerie.

"There's no last name," Mrs. Hankins said.

"I know who it is," Ruth Ellen said quietly. She looked at the card with the fancy finishing school signature and then tucked it in among the roses. "Yes, send these to the church," she said.

The altar of Trinity Episcopal Church was banked with flowers and organ music played softly. Nina stared directly ahead, her black lace mantilla half covering her face, a gold cross at her throat, numb, drained of all blood, her eyes dry. It all had an air of unreality, a dreadful dreamlike quality, and yet she knew it was not a dream.

Lathrop on one side of her, Ruth Ellen on the other.

The people gathered here, those closest to Peter, and the absent ones who were here in spirit, and in the rear of the church and at each exit the law, a Texas Ranger scanning the mourners for the killer.

The minister stepped in front of the gray coffin with its white cross of white flowers and opened his prayer book. He looked out over the congregation and cleared his throat.

"I am the resurrection and the life saith the Lord: he that believeth in me, though he were dead, yet shall he live."

The church was warm and the air sickening sweet with the scent of stock and tuberoses. Nina started to feel faint and gripped the pew for support.

"The Lord gave and the Lord hath taken away. . . ."

Ruth Ellen sobbing quietly, Lathrop blowing his nose.

Outside the black hearse waiting, newspaper reporters, the curious, witness to their private tragedy.

"Peter . . . Peter," she whispered.

Easter, a church filled with lilies. Peter and Marcia holding their mite boxes, dimes and nickels saved during Lent.

"What are you going to give up for Lent, Peter?"

A pause. "Candy." The supreme sacrifice.

Jelly beans, chocolate bunnies, green cellophane grass, yellow marshmallow chicks, colored eggs hidden in the azalea bushes and behind trees. "Look how many I found!" One Easter Peter had a real bunny, and another time live chicks. They didn't live long.

Nothing lives long, only memories.

"I will lift up mine eyes until the hills, from whence cometh my help. . . ."

"Look, Mummy, you can see a beautiful scene in this egg. You have to hold it up to the light."

Spring, summer, another year.

"But all the other boys are wearing long pants. This suit makes me look like a sissy!"

Peter, I don't want you to grow up too soon. You have all the rest of your life. Enjoy your childhood. It never comes back. It never comes back. . . .

"Let us pray. Remember thy servant, Peter, O Lord. . . ."

Peter's confirmation in the National Cathedral. How handsome he looks in his new dark suit!

"Look, Marcia, aren't you proud of your brother?"

A shrug. "Is it over now?"

"Almost."

Baptism, confirmation, death. No, she had forgotten the marriage ceremony, between confirmation and death. Like stepping stones down a garden path, flowers changing with the seasons, rain, sunshine, weeds growing between the stones, life was all of these, and you went on, somehow you went on.

"The Lord lift up his countenance upon you, and give you peace, both now and evermore. Amen."

Peace. As long as Peter's killer was alive, she would never have peace. And even if they found him, nothing could bring Peter back to life. Peter, my beloved son. . . .

Next to her Ruth Ellen was crying, Lathrop trying in vain to comfort her. She knew she should reach out her hand to her, but she couldn't bring herself to do it. If it hadn't been for her, if he hadn't come to this godforsaken place, none of this would have happened. If only he had married Valerie instead. . . .

Nina stared straight ahead, alone with her thoughts.

TWENTY-FOUR

*S*hould she have sent the flowers? Valerie wondered. But why not? He was a man she had loved, had almost married, whose child she would have had if. . . .

Why didn't she tell him? Would things have turned out differently if she had? Too late now. Now another woman, a woman she did not know, was to bear his child, the only child he would ever have, one that he would never see.

For Peter was dead, buried, the funeral was over. Last night she had dreamed of him again. But what good are dreams? He was gone from her life now forever.

A Texas sheriff had called her, asked her questions, but there was nothing she could tell him. She had no idea of anyone who would have wanted to kill Peter. Was he engaged in any questionable activities? None that she knew of, but then she had not seen him for two years. There was nothing in his past that she could recall that would lead to his death in a Texas oil town by an unknown assailant.

But someone had wanted him dead, enough to make several attempts, and finally he had succeeded, whoever he was. Or her. That had not occurred to her before. It could have been a woman.

Peter's life since he left for Midland was a mystery to her, other than a few brief letters.

I could have prevented what happened if I had gone out there the way he wanted me to, we would have been together, he would be alive now.

The thought tortured her. But was she really responsible? Was his death fate, written in a book long ago, so that there was no choice? She remembered the time he told her about a French family who had befriended him during the war and that they promised to put flowers on his grave if he was killed.

"You were not meant to die then," she had said.

"No, I guess not."

Later. He was meant to survive the war, but die only a few years later.

Or was it just that he was in the wrong place at the wrong time? No, Peter's death was not chance. Someone stalked him, wanted him out of the way, for some reason she could not imagine.

"Valerie, fifteen minutes," the stage manager called.

Her mascara was running. She took a tissue and blotted it, then applied some more.

What had happened had happened. It was over and there was nothing she could do about it. She had loved Peter but she hadn't wanted to be just a housewife in Midland, Texas. And her career won out. It would sustain her now, see her through, tragedy would make her a better actress.

"Five minutes, Valerie."

"Thank you. I'm ready."

"What time is your plane?" Lathrop asked.

"Two-thirty," Nina said.

"I'll drive you to the airport."

"That won't be necessary. I can take a cab."

Why was she always so difficult? "I'd like to," he said.

"Oh, all right."

They were sitting in the Scharbauer Hotel coffee shop. Nina was still dressed in black with a large picture hat. Several oilmen coming into the coffee shop turned to stare at her. She could always stop traffic, Lathrop thought.

"I'll be so glad to get out of this place," Nina said. "How much longer are you going to stay?"

"I'm not sure. A week or more. Until I find out something."

"Has that private investigator come up with anything useful?"

"Not much, but I guess it takes time. Don't worry, I intend to get to the bottom of it."

"I still can't imagine. . . ." Her voice trailed off.

"I know."

"It still seems so unreal."

"At least there will be the baby."

"The what?"

"Peter's child. His and Ruth Ellen's."

Nina stiffened.

"Our grandchild." She doesn't care anything about the coming baby, he thought. Maybe after he's born she will feel differently. If not, at least he'll have a grandfather who's interested in him. Or if it's a girl, that will be fine too. Nina never was very maternal, he recalled, pushing Peter and Marcia off on Fräulein, hardly seeing them.

Nina was staring into space.

Why did he still love her after everything? Looking at her across the table all other women paled, he was like a hungry dog begging to be thrown a bone and he hated himself for his lack of pride. But why must she still be so damnably beautiful?

"Let's get out of here," Nina said. "I still have to pack. And I want to place a call to Roberto so he'll know what time to meet me."

Of course. She had to rub that in. "I'll get the check," Lathrop said.

❖

There were dark thunderclouds as they approached the airport.

"It looks like a storm," Nina said. "I hope my flight won't be delayed. If it is, I'll miss my connection at Dallas."

"I think you'll be able to take off," Lathrop said.

"What a horrible little airport it is! I wonder if they even have radar?"

"I'm sure they do. There are oilmen flying in and out of here all the time in private planes."

"Thank God I'll never have to come here again!"

Then she doesn't intend to see the baby. Would he ever see her again after today? And yet they would share a grandchild, probably the only one they would ever have, the same flesh and blood. . . .

"You'll let me know if they find out anything? About who killed Peter and why?"

"Of course." He pulled up in front of the airport. "I'll let you out here and then park the car."

"That's all right. I'll just go on in. My plane will be leaving in a few minutes. I wonder if they have porters in this damned place?"

He unlocked the trunk and took out her suitcases.

"Porter?" Nina snapped her fingers at a passing man.

"No, ma'am. But I'll be glad to carry your bags. I'm taking the flight to Dallas myself."

"I don't want to trouble you."

"No trouble." He looked at Lathrop and picked up Nina's suitcases. "I'll see that your wife gets safely on the plane."

"That's very kind of you." He leaned over and kissed Nina on the cheek and the scent of "Bellodgia" wafted up his nostrils. She pulled away. "Have a good flight, Nina."

You'll manage, he thought, watching her disappear into the airport, the oilman carrying her bags with a smitten expression. Nina could charm anyone when she wanted to.

There was a bitter taste in his mouth. Why do we cling to the dream when the dream has turned to ashes? He got back in his car and started the engine, thinking how much he wanted a drink. Several drinks, good stiff ones. But he was taking Ruth Ellen out to dinner and he had to stay sober until later. Then he could drink himself into a stupor.

The car was swerving to one side and the left wheel was making a strange noise. He pulled to the side of the highway and got out to inspect it. Just then he saw a black Cadillac with steer horns on the front speeding down the road. It was coming right at him and for a moment he felt frozen to the spot, as if in a nightmare, and then his reflexes worked and he jumped out of the way just in time.

Was it deliberately trying to hit him?

The black Cadillac disappeared in a cloud of dust. It had been going so fast that he wasn't able to get the license number, but the car looked familiar. He wondered where he had seen it before.

He got back in his car. These rental cars they gave you were always lousy. The left rear wheel was loose, but he thought if he drove carefully he could make it back to town and a garage.

❖

Missed him that time, thought Earl Copeland, swearing to himself, but I'll get him yet. No one gets away from old Earl. He should have gone back home after his son's funeral and not started poking around in things with that private investigator he'd hired in New York. Leave things that happen in Texas to Texans. The sheriff hadn't come up with anything and wasn't likely to, and it would just die out as another of those unsolved murders if Lathrop Spaulding hadn't started stirring up trouble. He intended to stop him in his tracks.

And he'd just missed him by inches. The perfect chance, he was busy inspecting the car wheel, there was hardly any traffic on the highway, if only Spaulding hadn't turned around and jumped out of the way.

The black Cadillac with steer horns continued to speed toward town and half an hour later pulled up in front of the Petroleum Club.

❖

"Did Peter's mother get off all right?" Ruth Ellen asked, when Lathrop appeared at the house just as the rain was pouring down.

"Yes, she should be in Dallas by now," Lathrop said.

"She's very beautiful."

Yes, Nina was that, he thought.

"But not very . . . friendly. I don't think she cared for me very much."

Lathrop put his arm around Ruth Ellen. "That's just the way she is. Don't let it bother you."

"But it does. I want her to like me."

Nina dispensed love when she wanted to, but there was no need to say that to Ruth Ellen. "I'm sure she likes you. She was just upset."

"Yes, I guess so. Maybe she'll be friendlier after the baby's born. I hope she'll come back for a visit."

Nina would never return to Midland, that he knew, and she would certainly not invite Ruth Ellen to Rio de Janeiro. How could he explain Nina's complicated emotional makeup to this girl who was so open and trusting, so utterly without guile? But then he had never understood Nina completely and perhaps that was part of the fascination she still held for him. The eternal mystery woman.

Ruth Ellen looked out the window. "It's raining the same way it was the night Peter. . . ."

"Now, let's go and have a good dinner," Lathrop said, trying to divert her. "I had to trade in my car at the rental agency and pick up another one, so we're a little late, but I'm sure they'll hold the reservation. Do you have your raincoat?"

"I'll go get it."

❖

"Did you ever meet Valerie?" Ruth Ellen asked him over dinner. "Valerie?"

"A friend of Peter's from Washington." She watched his face carefully for a sign. "She sent yellow roses to the funeral."

"Oh, yes, Valerie Blair." He paused. "I met her once. It was several years ago."

"Was she pretty?"

"Yes, as I recall. Why do you ask?"

"I just wondered," she said vaguely. There was something he was not telling her but she decided not to pursue it. "It wasn't important."

"You're not eating much," he said, looking at her plate. "Would you like to order something else instead?"

"Oh, no, this is fine."

"This place was recommended to me as one of the best restaurants in Midland."

"It is. And everything is delicious. It's just that I don't have much of an appetite."

"I know. But you have to keep up your strength."

"That's what Mrs. Hankins keeps telling me."

"She's right."

She poked her food around and took a few bites. "I'm so glad you're here, Dad. You've been so good to me."

He smiled. "That's not hard to do."

"I don't know how I'd have managed without you."

"I'll be around whenever you need me," he said. "You just have to pick up the phone and I can hop on a plane. And when the baby is big enough, you both can come visit me in New York."

"I've never been to New York."

"Then it's about time. I'll show you Rockefeller Center, the zoo, we can ride in a horse and buggy around Central Park, and then we'll go to F.A.O. Schwarz, the best toy store in the world, and I'll buy him whatever he wants."

She laughed. "You'll probably spoil him to death. Or her."

"Of course. Isn't that what grandfathers are for?"

"You've made me feel a lot better."

"Good. Then let's order some dessert."

TWENTY-FIVE

When Lathrop returned to the hotel there was a message to call an operator in Reno, and he suddenly realized that in his grief over Peter he had completely forgotten Marcia. He should have telephoned her right after the funeral and he meant to, he thought guiltily, but somehow it had slipped his mind. He poured himself a stiff drink and then picked up the phone and asked for the Reno operator.

Marcia had gone out so he left his number for her to call him as soon as she returned and then he had another drink and another after that and finally the amber liquid was drained from the bottle and he no longer cared about anything.

He dreamed that he was in a plane trying to take off in a heavy fog and the plane was going so slowly. All the other passengers were tightly strapped in their seats, but he was seated in a wicker chair.

An insistent bell ringing through the fog awakened him and he reached out groggily for the phone and mumbled something into it.

"Dad . . . Dad? Are you there? It's Marcia."

"Marcia? I tried to get you earlier."

"Yes, I got your message. Are you all right? You sound strange."

"I must have fallen asleep. What time is it?"

"It's one o'clock. I wouldn't have phoned at this hour but you said to call as soon as I got in."

"It's all right. I wanted to talk to you." His words slurred. "Good old Marcia. The brick. Remember I used to call you that?"

"Dad, you sound as if you've been drinking. Is Mother still there?"

"I took your mother to the airport this afternoon."

"How is she?"

"The same."

"I mean how is she holding up?"

"Better than I am."

"It must have been awful for you, Peter's funeral and everything. How much longer are you going to stay in Midland?"

"Until I find the bastard who killed my son."

"Do they have any leads?"

"No, nothing definite. But I'll find him."

"Dad, maybe I should come on down there as soon as I have my divorce hearing."

"When will that be?"

"A week from Monday."

"Good. You'll finally be rid of that phony."

"Miklos had some good points, Dad. And I loved him. At least in the beginning. . . ." Her voice broke suddenly and he heard a muffled sob.

"I'm sorry, Marcia," he said quickly. "I didn't mean that."

"Yes you did. I know you never liked Miklos."

"Well can you blame me?" Women were strange, he thought. They cared more for a man who was a heel than one who treated them decently. Nina's face floated before his eyes as she walked away from him in the airport and out of his life once more. "I understand how you feel, Marcia, really I do."

"Do you, Dad? I feel like such a failure that I couldn't make it work."

"It wasn't your fault. You mustn't blame yourself." And it wasn't mine either with Nina, he thought, but the dream died hard. "We just had bad luck," he said. "Both of us."

"You still love Mother, don't you?"

"It wasn't easy seeing her again."

"That's what scares me. Maybe I'll never get over Miklos, maybe I'll never trust any man again or feel anything for anyone."

"Of course you will. It takes time." That was a lie, he thought, that saying that time healed everything. Time had not healed his wounds, but he had to give her some hope.

"How is Ruth Ellen?"

"She's a sweet girl. You two should get to know each other. I think you'd like her."

"I'm sure I would." She paused. "How did Mother behave? Was she nice to her?"

"In her way. As much as she was able."

"I was hoping I could speak to Mother, that she would call me when she was there, but I guess she didn't have time."

"I'm sure she intended to, but she was so distraught about Peter."

"I know. It's awful. I still can't believe it."

You'd believe it if you'd seen his body the way I did, he thought, battered and filled with bullet holes. I'm glad you didn't. His throat started to constrict and he felt as if he couldn't swallow.

"Dad? Are you still there?"

He coughed and tried to clear his throat. He felt as if giant hands were squeezing him around the neck. He coughed again. "Just hang on a minute. I want to get a drink of water." He went into the bathroom and ran the cold water tap and filled a glass and took several swallows. Better. He drained the glass and returned to the phone. "I had something in my throat," he said. "I thought I was going to choke."

"Are you all right now?"

"Yes, fine. Did you say you might come on down here?"

"I was thinking about it. I could check on plane flights and let you know."

"And what are your plans after that? Are you going back to New York?"

"No, I'd planned to go to San Francisco and visit an old school friend for about a week. Do you remember Phoebe Harkness who went to Foxcroft with me?"

"Can't say that I do."

"Well, Phoebe has invited me to come and stay with her. Her family has a place in Burlingame. And after that I'm not sure. I might just get on a freighter to the South Seas and drift from port to port with no destination. I've never been out that way before and it would be a change."

That's what I'd like to do, Lathrop thought, get away from everything. "Sounds like a good idea," he said.

"I've heard that those freighters take only a few passengers and are quite comfortable. . . ." Her voice trailed off.

Once he and Nina had talked about taking a cruise to Tahiti and Fiji and some of those South Sea islands, chartering a yacht, but then something had come up and they never went. "Call me back when you find out about flights to Midland," he said.

"I will, Dad."

"Goodnight, daughter. It was good talking to you." He hung up the phone.

Now he was wide awake and he didn't have anything with him to read himself to sleep. He should have picked up a good Western in a drugstore. He opened the drawer of his bedside table and found nothing but a Gideon Bible. He started to close the drawer, then changed his mind and opened the Bible and idly turned the pages. Maybe if he closed his eyes and put his finger on a passage at random it would give him a direction, an answer about what to do with the rest of his life. Except for dabbling around in the stock market and investing in several businesses that had failed, he hadn't done very much. The curse of inherited money.

When he got back to New York he should start going to Sunday services at St. Bartholomew's, his old church, take communion again. How long had it been since he had done that, received the body and blood of Christ? Suddenly something his mother had once said about the communion service came back to him. "I like to think of it as being invited to a tea party." She told him that the idea about receiving the body and blood of Christ repulsed her. Strange, he had not thought of that remark in years and he remembered how startled he had been when she made it. It was right after he was confirmed and had the symbolic body and blood of Christ for the first time.

He turned to the psalms and started to read the 121st Psalm. "I will lift up mine eyes unto the hills, from whence cometh my help." It had been a favorite of his mother's. "My help cometh from the Lord, which made heaven and earth."

He continued to read the psalm over and over again until finally his eyes closed and he fell asleep.

He dreamt that Peter was a baby again being christened at St. Bartholomew's and Nina was there beside him, and his mother, wearing a large garden hat trimmed with flowers, was pouring tea at the communion altar. Instead of an Episcopal minister a Catholic priest was holding the baby and when Lathrop looked into his face he was startled to recognize Roberto Carvalho.

"Cast out the devil!" the priest said, sprinkling holy water on the baby. "Cast out the devil!"

His mother continued to pour tea from the communion urn into tiny china cups. "Do you take cream or lemon in your tea?" she asked.

TWENTY-SIX

The pains started in the middle of the night and Ruth Ellen gripped the sheets, her palms wet with perspiration, thinking: The baby's not due for another three weeks.

The pains came closer and closer together. Finally she could stand it no longer and called out for Mrs. Hankins.

Mrs. Hankins came quickly, a robe hastily thrown on over her nightgown, her hair in a long gray braid down her back. She took one look at Ruth Ellen's white, drawn face, her hands clenching and unclenching the sheets, and called Doc Kelsey.

"He says to get to the hospital right away and he'll meet you there."

Ruth Ellen nodded weakly and tried to stand up. "I'll get dressed." Suddenly there was a fierce pain, stronger than any of the others, and then she felt warm water gushing down her legs. "Mrs. Hankins," she called, "I think the waters have broken."

Mrs. Hankins had thrown on some clothes and was pinning her hair back in a bun. "There's no time to lose," she said. "Let's go."

Ruth Ellen barely made it to the delivery room. There was a pain that seemed to tear her apart, then a cry, a sharp cry piercing the air, a strong, angry cry.

"A boy," she heard them say.

That was my baby crying, she thought. Our son, Peter's and mine. She smiled faintly.

"Would you like to see your baby?" Doc Kelsey asked. "He's a very nice little boy."

A red face with light brown hair. The eyes tightly shut, the tiny fist clenched.

"Determined little tyke," Doc Kelsey remarked.

"How much does he weigh?"

"We don't weigh them here. I'd say about six pounds."

We made it, she thought. He's all right. We have a son, Peter. We have a son.

She felt herself being lifted onto a cart. The sound of wheels as they rolled it through the corridors, a ride in an elevator with faces floating above her, another long corridor, and then her room. The clanking of metal bars as they fastened the guard rails around her bed, a nurse in a starched cap. A hypodermic needle.

"We want you to get some sleep."

"May I see my baby again?"

"Later. We'll bring him in later. You sleep now."

"Peter," she whispered. And then she drifted off.

Lathrop was sitting in a chair by her bed when she awoke.

"Have you seen him yet?" she asked.

"Yes. He's a fine little fellow."

There was an arrangement of pink roses and forget-me-nots by her bed and a small stuffed teddy bear.

"The flowers are from me," Lathrop said.

"Thank you, Dad. They're lovely."

"And I had to get something for my grandson. I wanted to get him a football, but he's a little young yet."

She smiled. "He is a nice baby, isn't he?"

"Perfect."

"If only Peter could have seen him." Tears filled her eyes.

Lathrop patted her hand awkwardly. "Now, now."

A nurse came in with a tray. "I'm afraid I'm going to have to ask you to leave now, Mr. Spaulding."

Lathrop got up. "See you later," he said, and left.

He must put a call through to Nina now and inform her of the news. She should be back in Rio de Janeiro now. Too bad she couldn't have stayed a little longer and then she would have seen her grandson, but who could have predicted that he would arrive prematurely? Well maybe it was predictable after the trauma Ruth Ellen had gone through.

Nina, you have a grandson. We have a grandson. How should he put it? Now that she was back with that bastard Carvalho, the man who had stolen her away from him, broken up his marriage. . . .

The green-eyed monster that would never let him go, who haunted his dreams. Was there any hate stronger than jealousy? In the beginning he had hoped that the marriage would not go well, that Carvalho would leave Nina as she had walked out on him. Then the circle would be complete, he would have his revenge. But apparently that was not in the cards. Nina still loved Carvalho, couldn't wait to get back to him. Who could define love? It crept up on you when you were not looking and locked you in its embrace, it defied all reason, it drove you insane.

He poured himself a drink and then asked the operator to put the call through to Rio de Janeiro.

Roberto answered the telephone. Nina was lying down and Doctor Silva had given her a sedative. She had arrived in a state of complete exhaustion after the long plane flight. Yes, he would give her the message. A boy, six pounds, eight ounces. His voice was cool, indifferent.

"Please ask her to call this number as soon as she can," Lathrop said.

"I will tell her." Roberto heard Nina stirring in the next room and abruptly he hung up the phone.

"Who was that?" she mumbled.

He walked into her room. Nina lay drugged under the pale green silk canopy. He looked down at her. "It was nothing important, *querida*." He kissed her on the forehead. "Now get some sleep. I will look in on you later."

Bastard! thought Lathrop. He doesn't intend to let me talk to Nina. I'll have to send her a cable to be sure that she gets the news. But Carvalho could intercept that too.

He walked over and looked out the window. There was a man standing on the curb looking up at his room and when he saw Lathrop he turned and lit a cigarette. A tail? Who would be tailing him and why? Someone who didn't want him to find out who had murdered Peter?

He'd take a shower and put on fresh clothes, then maybe he'd feel better. He opened a bureau drawer to get a shirt and suddenly he noticed that someone had gone through his things while he was out. He looked in his closet. The lock on his suitcase had been tampered with, but it appeared that whoever it was had been interrupted. At a quick glance he couldn't discover anything missing, but he didn't like the idea that someone had been in his room. Again.

Could it be that whoever had killed Peter was after him as well?

Perhaps he should hire a bodyguard for the rest of the time he was in Midland.

He'd pay the sheriff a visit and find out just what was going on.

❖

"Right glad you came by," Sheriff Mahoney said, offering Lathrop a cigar.

"No thanks. Have you found out anything?"

"Not much, but there are a few questions I wanted to ask you."

He glared at the sheriff sitting there so calmly puffing on his cigar. His office didn't seem in any hurry to solve Peter's murder. Could it be that someone had paid him off, someone high up? A sheriff of a small Texas town couldn't make that much. A bribe would probably be hard to turn down. "There are a few things I'd like to ask you, too," Lathrop said.

"Such as?"

"Someone is following me, my room has been searched, and a car tried to run me down on the highway. I'm beginning to think it's all connected, that someone wants this investigation stopped."

"Could be."

Lathrop exploded in fury. "Then what do you intend to do about it? Because I'm not leaving Midland until my son's killer is found and brought to justice."

"That's a pretty tall order, Mr. Spaulding. Like I said before, these things take time. And we don't have much evidence to go on. It's like a jigsaw puzzle, piece by piece, you keep looking, and then something fits."

"I want this solved within a week."

"I understand you have your own private investigator?"

"That's correct."

"And is he doing any better?"

Lathrop had to admit to himself that he was not. His eyes met Sheriff Mahoney's and then looked away.

"That's what I thought. Mr. Spaulding, we don't like these unsolved murders any better than you do. It don't look good on the record. Now. . . ." He picked up a note pad. "There are some names I want to ask you about."

No point in antagonizing the sheriff. "Yes?"

"Erna Schmidt."

Erna Schmidt. For a moment the name did not make sense. And then it came to him. Fräulein. The plain scrubbed face with the braid wound round her head. "She was my children's German nurse. We always called her Fräulein, never by her name."

"We have written to her in Germany, but we haven't had a reply."

"I haven't seen her in years. I'm not even sure she's still alive. But even so, she wouldn't know anything."

"Like I said, the jigsaw puzzle. Sometimes things that don't appear to have any connection lead to something."

"She was a good woman," Lathrop said, seeing her leaning over Peter during his asthma attacks. Much more devoted than Nina, he thought. "She adored Peter. She cried when she left."

"You fired her?"

"Not exactly. Peter was getting big and he was going off to summer camp. We just didn't need her anymore."

"We found a book of German fairy tales she had given him among his effects."

"He kept that book?" Lathrop remembered Fräulein reading it to Peter. Some of the stories were pretty scary and gave him nightmares. "That was a long time ago," he said. Suddenly he found his eyes filling with tears and he looked away. "A long time ago. . . ."

The doorbell rang at Erna Schmidt's home in Freudenstadt and she hurried to answer it. The postman stood on the doorstep waving a letter.

"Good morning, Heinz," she said. "I see you have mail for me."

"Good morning, Erna. Yes, I have a letter for you from America."

America. Could it be from—no, it was not possible, it had been too long, but she could not think of anyone else who would write to her from America other than her beloved little Peter. Eagerly she held out her hand for the letter.

"It is registered," Heinz said. "You must sign for it."

"So?" She looked at it. "It must be important." There was an official-looking seal. Office of the Sheriff, Midland, Texas. "I don't know anyone in Texas," she said as she signed the receipt.

Heinz was watching her with interest.

"Good day, Heinz," she said and closed the door. Heinz was a good man but a gossip and curious to know everyone's business so he could pass it on to the next person. But after all, in a small town like Freudenstadt, what else was there to do? It was not like living in Munich or even Hamburg where her brother Gottfried lived with his wife and children, leaving her with the complete responsibility of taking care of Mutti and waiting on her hand and foot and listening to her complaining day after day. Gottfried hardly ever sent money to help out with Mutti's needs, she thought bitterly, and she had almost exhausted her savings from her years of working in America.

"Erna," came her mother's whining voice calling from the garden. "You were going to get me my shawl. I want my shawl."

"Just a minute, Mutti."

Erna sat down in the chair next to a good light and tore open the letter. She read it slowly, translating it in her head from English into German for her English had gotten rusty in the years since she had left America. At first she was not quite sure if it said what she thought it did and then she let out an agonized scream.

"Mein Peter! Gott im Himmel!"

It was not true, it could not be true! She started to weep hysterically. How could this awful thing have happened to him, her little baby? She had taken such good care of him, she had loved him so much. Who would have wanted to kill her beloved Peter? And only twenty-eight years old!

Did they think that maybe she knew something? She knew nothing. Nothing. It was not possible to imagine who could have hated him. She thought a moment. Except possibly the stepfather. . . .

I should have taken you with me, my Peter, dressed you in lederhosen, kept you from harm. You were such a good little boy. Remember how I used to rock you in my arms when you were unable to sleep, tell you stories? Why did this have to happen to you, my little Peter. Your Fräulein loved you so much. I hoped that one day you would come to Germany and pay a visit to your old nurse.

Oh, my Peter, it is too much!

"Erna!" her mother yelled. "Get my shawl!"

"Oh, be quiet, Mutti. Leave me alone!"

"What did you say?"

"Just leave me alone!" And she burst into tears again.

TWENTY-SEVEN

Sheriff Mahoney put the file back in the cabinet and locked it. The little shreds of information they had seemed to be leading nowhere, and with each day that passed, the probability of finding Peter Spaulding's killer grew dimmer.

Unless someone talked.

But everyone he'd checked out had an alibi and there were no witnesses to the murder, no one driving by in the rain had come forth to describe a car, a license number, they couldn't even find a motive.

Every murder had a motive and once you found out who had a reason to want the victim dead, you worked from there, spreading out in an ever-widening circle until the trap was sprung.

Earl Copeland. He scribbled the name on a pad in front of him. That name had gone through his mind more than once, but what reason would he have for wanting Peter Spaulding dead? And he wasn't anywhere near the scene at the time of the murder, he'd verified that. Of course he could have hired someone to do it, but why? There were rumors going around town that Copeland intended to run for governor, so he didn't need no skeletons in his closet to be dragged out come election time.

He'd also heard that Copeland had a mistress, what with his

wife being an invalid, but a mistress was one thing and any man could understand that in his situation. Murder was something else.

No, Earl Copeland was far too smart to get himself mixed up in a murder.

He crossed out the name and spat into the spittoon. This case was getting to him, and unless someone talked, it didn't look like it was ever going to be solved.

The phone rang and he picked it up. "Mahoney." It was the Texas Ranger. "How ya doin' this mornin'?" He scratched his head. "Yeah?" He listened, taking notes, disappointment clouding his face. Nothing new. "We'll check it out. Thanks."

Another useless lead, he thought, putting down the phone. He'd heard that the wife had a little boy. He should go by and see her, bring her some flowers. She must be feelin' mighty alone now. Didn't know how he'd gotten more involved in this case than the others, but he had. The rest he just put in the file cabinet and forgot.

His deputy knocked on the door. Another Mexican arrested on a drug charge. These guys couldn't stay out of trouble.

He thought of the bellboy, what was his name . . . Manuel? Yeah, that was it. The one from the Scharbauer, the one they found knifed in the alley. Thought that might lead to something, but it hadn't. Another dead end.

The Mexican in handcuffs was glaring at him.

"Arraign him," Sheriff Mahoney said to the deputy.

"You're looking much better today," Lathrop said.

Ruth Ellen smiled. "I feel better." She pointed to an arrangement of daisies and bachelor buttons. "Sheriff Mahoney brought those by. Wasn't that sweet of him?"

Lathrop nodded. It would be sweeter if he'd solve who killed my son, he thought. Looks like he's got a crush on Ruth Ellen or something.

Ruth Ellen's face clouded. "There's been nothing from Peter's mother. You did get in touch with her, didn't you?"

"I've tried. That is, I've left messages. I'll call again when I get back to the hotel."

"Oh, that's all right. I just wondered why I hadn't heard anything."

Either Nina doesn't care, or that bastard Carvalho had kept the messages from her. Lathrop clenched his fist and perspiration started to run down his face. He'd better take one of his pills.

"I'll just go down to the water cooler," he said.

"Oh, you can get a glass in the bathroom." She pointed. "In there."

"Thanks."

He filled the glass and gulped his pill. He thought he had the seizures under control and then something triggered one, some emotion. . . . He felt a sudden desire to kill Carvalho, to put his hands on the throat of that slimy Brazilian, to close them around it until he stopped breathing. He put the glass back on the sink and took several deep breaths.

"Are you all right, Dad?" Ruth Ellen called.

"Fine." He came over and sat down on the chair beside her bed. "And how's my grandson doing?"

"He's gained weight." Ruth Ellen beamed. "And he's not as red as he was."

"Good, good."

"I want to ask Doc Kelsey if I can't go home tomorrow."

"Isn't that too soon?" How long had Nina stayed in the hospital with Peter and Marcia? He wasn't sure, but he thought it had been at least a week.

"I'll have Mrs. Hankins to take care of me and the baby. And I hate hospitals."

"I don't blame you."

"Though everyone here has been very nice."

Lathrop got up. "I think I'll walk down to the nursery and have another look at my grandson."

"Do you think he looks like Peter?"

"It's too soon to tell. But he's a fine little fellow." He leaned over and kissed her. "You get some more rest now. I'll see you tomorrow."

That night, sleep for Lathrop was elusive. But finally it caught up with him.

Nina was a mermaid with long hair wound with seed pearls and a green tail. At one bare breast she suckled a baby. She sat on a rock singing a lullaby, a Portuguese song whose words he could not understand. Waves beat on the rock, she smiled a mysterious smile, he reached out to her in his dream, she continued to sing, ignoring him.

With a start, he awoke.

A shadowy figure was standing at his window.

"What do you want?" Lathrop called.

The figure vanished.

Was it really there? Or had he only imagined it?

The black Cadillac with steer horns on front pulled into the garage of an expensive modern home on the outskirts of Midland and a heavy-set man with a sunburned face got out. He opened the front door with his keys and closed it as quietly as possible, then tiptoed down the hall. There was a light burning in Jo Beth's room.

"Earl? Is that you?" called a woman's voice.

"You should be asleep, Jo Beth."

"You know I can't sleep till you come home." She tried to raise herself in bed as Earl entered the room, then fell back on the pillow. "Where were you?"

"Now you know better than to ask that question."

"But I'm asking it. I lie here alone night after night—"

"I had business to take care of."

"Business! That's what you always say."

"We're not going to start that again, are we?" He looked down at her. For better or worse. They never told you that worse was what it turned into. Once she had been pretty, she laughed at his jokes, was interested in his work. Was that only before they were married? It seemed as if he had been married forever. Well, they had gotten married pretty young, they had been high school sweethearts. He hadn't intended to get married but she told him she was pregnant, and then the kid died, she got multiple sclerosis. . . .

"I wish I were dead," she said. "I might as well be."

"Now, now, Jo Beth. I don't want to hear you talk like that ever again. Ya hear me?"

"There's no cure for this disease. I'll just get worse and worse."

He was surprised that she had lived this long with it but he didn't say so. Instead he sat down on the bed and took her hand. "Go to sleep."

"I don't blame you for having other women."

Once he had loved her, or thought he did. But love had died a long time ago. Who was it who had said that power was the greatest aphrodisiac? In his case, it was true. He was going to be governor of this state and nothing and no one was going to stop him.

"All that's important to me is your getting well," he lied. "Now try and get a good night's sleep. I'll see you in the morning."

And he turned quickly away and walked down the hall to his bedroom.

TWENTY-EIGHT

*A*nother life beginning, a small hand reaching out in trust, what lies ahead for you, Peter my grandson? Babies are born with only two instincts, fear of falling and—what was the other one? Fear of the dark? He could not recall. Everything else, they said, was learned. Lathrop looked at the tiny baby in Ruth Ellen's arms. A new life, a new hope. The future there, all unwritten. Peter was dead. His son was dead and no one could bring him back, but his blood went on, his name continued.

"Wouldn't you like to hold him?" Ruth Ellen asked.

She held out the baby and Lathrop took him in his arms. Had Peter ever been this small? It seemed like such a long time ago. Twenty-eight years. He felt tears coming into his eyes.

"He's really quite strong," Ruth Ellen said. "You needn't be afraid."

The baby looked up at him with solemn blue eyes. Maybe he thinks I'm his father, Lathrop thought. He knew men in their fifties who married again, started new families. He looked across the hospital bed at Ruth Ellen. He would see that she had everything she needed and as soon as he got back to New York he would call his attorney about having a trust fund set up for little Peter, insure that he had a college education. Yale, class of 1970. Would he live long enough to see his grandson graduate from college? And what would the world be like then? Would his grandson be able to pursue his dreams in peace and not have to go off to war as his father had done?

The baby screwed up his face and started to cry.

"I think he's hungry," Ruth Ellen said.

Lathrop handed him back. "I'll be going along now." He had to check with Jake Birney and see if there was anything new. He was his only hope. That sheriff certainly didn't seem to be doing very much to solve Peter's murder. "When did the doctor say that you could go home?"

"The day after tomorrow."

"Good. Is there anything I can bring you?"

"No thanks, Dad. I'm fine."

"I'll be at the hotel if you need me." He wanted to try to get in touch with Nina again. It had been three days now since he left that message with Carvalho. She could at least send flowers and show some interest in the baby. After all, it was her grandson too. Or was that the problem? Didn't she want to admit that she was old enough to have a grandchild? There was no figuring out the way Nina's mind worked and he had long ago stopped trying.

That bastard Carvalho! He had ruined everything, he had cast a spell over Nina.

Just as she had cast one over him, from the first day he saw her in the green dress with the dangling earrings dancing the Charleston. . . .

He walked out of the hospital into the blinding summer sun of Midland, cursing under his breath.

Nina answered the phone.

"Did you get my message?" Lathrop asked. "The one I left three days ago?"

"No. Have they found out who. . . ."

"Not yet. But you have a grandson. I thought you'd want to know."

There was a quick intake of breath.

"Did you hear what I said?"

"Yes. But the baby wasn't due until. . . ."

"He came early. He's a fine little boy. I called you three days ago right after I came back from the hospital."

"Roberto must have forgotten to tell me."

"Ruth Ellen is doing all right, considering everything. They're going home the day after tomorrow, in case you want to send something." He waited.

There was a long pause. "Yes. Yes, of course."

He could hear a man's voice in the background and then Nina said, "Thank you for calling."

"Don't you want to know the baby's name?"

"What is it?"

"Peter."

"Peter," she repeated dully.

And then he heard her start to sob and the telephone was abruptly disconnected.

"Who was that on the telephone?" Roberto asked.

"It was Lathrop." Nina looked at him accusingly. "Why didn't you give me the message?"

"Which message?"

"He said he called three days ago and left a message to call him."

"*Querida*, I am sorry. I must have forgotten."

"You didn't forget."

"I did not want to upset you." He put his arms around her. "You were feeling better and—"

She pushed him away. "I have a grandson."

"But—"

"The baby came early." She glared at him. "Three days ago."

His face was expressionless. I know you don't like children, she thought. Strange. Most men want at least a son to carry on the family name. Roberto had been a bachelor for so long when she married him. Did he have illegitimate children somewhere? She knew he had had mistresses and she was sure she had met some of them at parties from the way they looked at him and his pretended aloofness. A surge of jealousy swept over her. Was there still someone, had there been anyone while she was in Midland? She had never felt the intense physical attraction for any man that she had for Roberto, for him she would have given up anything, everything. And she had.

"So you are a grandmother? You do not look any older, *querida*." He smiled.

"Do you still find me appealing?"

He reached out his arms. "Come here, my darling, and I will show you how much."

She went to him and they made love violently and passionately while the sky turned from pink to sapphire and the lights came on around Ipanema Bay. And she thought: This is all that matters. Nothing else.

Lathrop's mind again traveled the back roads of memory with Nina. Did he still love her or only regret loving her? What did it matter? He could not get her out of his mind.

Nina. A name that held magic and despair for him.

She lived in another world now, she had built herself a new life, while he walked on the burnt-out coals of the old one. He poured himself another drink but it didn't help. Her face kept appearing before him with a taunting smile.

Suddenly his head started to throb. Had he taken his pill? He couldn't remember, but it was too late now, he knew this feeling all too well, this sense of separation from everything as an aura of lights flashed across his eyes and his brain seemed on fire. He fell to the floor gasping for breath, his body jerking in convulsions, his jaw clenching and unclenching. His mouth filled with saliva and bloody froth trickled from his lips, the room whirled around him, and then he felt himself losing control of his bladder as he lapsed into unconsciousness.

When he finally awoke it was with a sense of confusion and panic. He had no idea where he was or what day it was. He was soaking wet and there was a strong smell of urine. Slowly it dawned on him that he had had one of his epileptic seizures. He heard someone knocking on the door and then the key turned in the lock and the maid came in with towels over her arm.

She gasped when she saw him lying on the floor and he tried to tell her he was all right, but his speech was so broken and he was stuttering so badly that he could not form a coherent sentence. She dropped the towels and ran from the room.

He raised himself to a sitting position. Sometimes one attack triggered another. He must be careful. He reached out for the chair and his legs felt rubbery as he tried to stand. Steady now, he told himself, take it easy. He walked slowly to the bathroom and splashed cold water in his face and rinsed out his mouth. What day was it and how long had he been lying there? He heard a knock on the door. The maid had returned with a man. A doctor? he wondered. He looked familiar somehow, but he couldn't place him.

"I'm Glen Phillips," the man said. "Assistant manager."

"Oh, yes."

"We met the other evening. Is everything all right?"

"F-f-fine, th-thank you," Lathrop tried to control his stammer as Phillips looked at him oddly.

"We were worried about you. No one had seen you come out of your room for more than a day and you weren't answering the telephone."

Lathrop waved his hand nonchalantly. "It's nothing."

The assistant manager glanced at the empty bottle of bourbon on the night table and then back at Lathrop, his eyes saying everything.

"Th-thank you for your concern," Lathrop said. "And now I'd like to take a shower if you don't mind."

"Just wanted to check. If you need anything, let me know. I'd be glad to be of service." And he backed out of the room followed by the maid.

Damn them all! Lathrop thought, as he locked the door securely and put on the safety chain.

The phone rang and he picked up the receiver.

"Dad, it's Marcia. I've been trying to reach you, but there wasn't any answer. And I left two messages—"

"I took a sleeping pill and I guess I didn't hear the phone," Lathrop said, thinking that was as good a story as any. "I just woke up."

"I almost called the hotel manager to see if you were all right."

"I'm fine," he said, wondering if Ruth Ellen or anyone else had tried to get him.

"Anyway, I've been checking with different airlines on plane schedules to Midland, and it's not the easiest place in the world to get to."

"You have to fly to Dallas first and then take a smaller plane to Midland."

"Yes, I know, but getting to Dallas from here isn't that simple. First I have to fly to Salt Lake City and change for a flight to Denver, wait there six hours—"

"Look, I won't be here more than a few days. Why don't you go to San Francisco and visit your friend the way you planned and then take your freighter cruise, and I'll see you back in New York when you return."

"You're sure?" Marcia's voice sounded relieved.

"Yes. There's no point in your coming here."

"Have you found out yet who killed Peter?"

"No, but I'm not going to stay here indefinitely. I've had about all I can take of this place."

"You're sure you're all right? I'm worried about you."

"Don't be. I'm perfectly all right. You just go ahead with your plans."

"If you say so. But take care of yourself, Dad."

"I will."

"I love you, Dad. Goodbye."

"Goodbye, Marcia. I love you too."

TWENTY-NINE

"I've got some news for you," Jake Birney said. He paused. "Is it all right to come up?"

"Fine," said Lathrop. "I'm alone." He hung up the phone with a shiver of apprehension. Was this just another false lead, or had that private investigator really found out who had murdered Peter? His hands were perspiring and then he started to tremble. Better take one of his pills. He'd probably need one when he heard what Birney had to say. He went into the bathroom and washed a pill down with a glass of water and then he heard a knock on the door.

He opened it. Birney walked in carrying a large manila envelope and took out some notes.

"You found out who did it?" Lathrop asked, beads of perspiration forming on his upper lip. He wiped them away with his hand.

Birney sat down. "Yeah. For all the good it does."

"What do you mean?"

"I mean they'll never put the finger on him because he's too powerful in this town."

"Not the sheriff?"

"Naw, he just does what he's told. A paid servant, so to speak. Oil runs this town, not the law."

"Go on."

"Earl Copeland. An oil man with political aspirations."

"He shot my son?" A vein throbbed in his left temple and he felt dizzy. "What for?"

"I'm coming to that. And I didn't say he did the shooting. He's too smart for that. Got a hired killer. Fellow's probably safe in Mexico by now. They'll never find him."

"Then it wasn't the bellboy?"

"No, but he knew something. He was bragging in a bar, and I guess they were afraid he was going to spill the beans."

"How did you learn all this?"

"I have my ways." He grinned slyly. "Newspaper men know a lot more than they put in the papers. And there's a Ranger who likes publicity. I told him I was writing a book."

"Why didn't Sheriff Mahoney come up with all this?"

"Like I said, he's running scared for election. And this Copeland's got a hell of a lot of power in these parts. It pays the sheriff to look the other way sometimes."

"What would have been the motive?" Lathrop was beginning to feel sick. "He had to have a reason to kill Peter."

"Oh, he had a reason all right. Your son knew too much about an illegal oil deal and he was going to tip off the boys in Washington. That's when Copeland decided to get rid of him. A dead man tells no tales."

Birney seemed to be enjoying these revelations. Mission accomplished. He was the star actor delivering the climactic monologue of the play.

"And there was a woman mixed up in it, a redhead. A two-bit nightclub singer and hoofer. Copeland's mistress. He has an invalid wife, and after all, a man's a man—"

"What does all this have to do with my son?"

"This Billie took a shine to your son and Copeland found out about it. They were having an affair and someone talked. Copeland travels a lot, so—"

"What was the illegal oil deal you mentioned? Was Peter involved in that?"

"Yeah, they used him as a front. He apparently thought it was on the up and up at first—you have to get up pretty early to beat these wheelers and dealers in the oil business—then he wanted to clear himself and that was where he made a mistake, he should've kept quiet."

"Was this before he started to work for Stanolind?"

Birney glanced at his notes. "He was kind of moonlighting. Stanolind's a legitimate outfit but they don't pay much. This other was a get-rich-quick deal."

He was glad Nina wasn't here, or Ruth Ellen. What good would it do to try to bring Peter's killer to justice? It would only serve to bring out all these sordid details. The tabloids would have a field day. Better to leave it as it was. Unsolved. To pursue this wouldn't bring Peter back to life, it would only blacken his name.

"I'll give you the money for your plane ticket back to New York and the rest of what I owe you," Lathrop said. He wanted Birney out of here. He had heard enough.

"Oh, I can find out a lot more if I stick around," Birney said.

Sure, he was getting paid a hundred dollars a day plus expenses. Why not drag out the case as long as he could? "I don't care to continue the investigation," Lathrop said. "And may I have those notes?"

"Why . . . sure, if you want."

He would get rid of them as soon as Birney left, tear them in small pieces and flush them down the toilet. There would be no bits of paper left in a wastebasket to be found by a maid or someone and glued together. Case closed. He stood up, glaring at Birney.

Birney reluctantly handed him the notes. "Well, if that's the way you want it, Mr. Spaulding. I sure am sorry about your son and all." He fingered the cash greedily and put it in his wallet. "You have my card. If ever I can be of service—"

"Get out!"

"Sure, sure." He left quickly, glancing over his shoulder as if he expected Lathrop to hit him.

Lathrop sank down in the armchair by the window and put his head in his hands. He turned out the light. In this dark lonely hotel room he felt as if he had come to the end of the world and there was no hope anywhere. Everything he had dreamed of, all his plans for the future, were over.

He did not know how long he sat there. Finally he took Birney's notes and tore them into shreds and flushed them down the toilet.

THIRTY

T he night sounds of New York drifted through the open bathroom window, he could hear taxis honking taking people to the theatre, ships on the river, laughter and music in the next apartment.

At fifty, Lathrop thought, a man should have accomplished the things he dreamed at eighteen. What had he done with his life? What had he contributed to eternity? He felt old and tired and empty. Fifty wasn't old. For some men it was the prime of life, the time when the hard work of their youth bore fruit, when their political ambitions were realized, if they had any. He had inherited money, he had never had to work hard, to struggle, to wonder where his next dime was coming from.

A life of no significance, that had been his. Why continue it? For what purpose?

He picked up the razor blade and ran his finger along the sharp edge, wondering if he would have the courage to do it.

Some said it took more courage to live than to die, to meet adversity head-on and rise above it. He turned on both faucets and watched the tub fill with water. Who would miss him? To whom was he really important?

The world is nothing but shadows and illusion, there is no

happiness that is not fleeting, no love that lasts.

He had loved Nina and she left him for another. Would she cry over him? He knew the answer to that.

He had thought of writing Nina a farewell note and then decided against it. Why give her that satisfaction? There were other women in the world, beautiful women, younger women, and he had had many of them, but they were only a temporary gratification for his physical needs. His soul hungered for Nina, she drifted in starlight through his sleepless nights, stretching out her arms to him, smiling tauntingly at him and then turning away. He smelled again the fragrance of carnations, she had him in her power, she had blotted out all other faces for him, the spell she cast would never be broken.

Well, he knew how to do that.

He took off his bathrobe and got in the tub. The water was warm. They said it didn't hurt in warm water, you couldn't feel anything. After the past few weeks it would be a relief not to feel anything. He picked up the razor.

The current was bearing him along now, irresistibly, the current of life against which he could no longer struggle, it was a raging river, a red river, red blood flowing. He watched the blood seep into the tub, he felt weak and drowsy, but there was no pain. I give you back the life you gave me, take it. Forgive me, Mother. Forgive. . . .

He closed his eyes. The river was warm . . . so warm . . . he was drifting . . . far . . . far off . . . he heard a roaring in his ears like rapids . . . and then the red waters engulfed him.

THIRTY-ONE

Marcia leaned on the railing of the deck as the freighter approached Bali. Dawn was rising over the Pacific and on the horizon there was the faint promise of sun shining through the silvery-blue clouds. A sailor climbed to the mast with ropes and the ship gave two long blasts and one short one. She watched the other ships in the harbor, a large white cruise ship, a Dutch freighter, several small boats. The sea was calm and now the sun burst through and a pale rose lined the clouds. Suddenly a small yellow bird flew into the wheelhouse, then frightened, flew out again and perched on a ladder.

For six weeks she had drifted, the sea cradling her like a womb, exotic strange ports distracting her tortured memories. Her divorce, Peter's murder, her father's suicide, it all blurred together like a half-remembered dream. Slowly she was getting herself together.

She could easily get used to freighter life, she thought, and become a permanent passenger. The food was good and the shipboard routine was casual with no dressing up. The seven other passengers included a couple from Oregon, a schoolteacher from Seattle, a retired doctor from Michigan, an ex-newspaper reporter who was writing a novel, and a real estate salesman from Albuquerque with his wife.

The doctor came over and stood beside her. "This is really the life, isn't it?" he said. "I wonder if they need another member of the crew."

Marcia laughed. "I was just wondering that myself."

"After Florence died I didn't know what to do with my time. Just sat around the house and moped, played a little golf. Then a friend told me about these freighter trips. I feel like a new person."

"Me too," Marcia said.

But sometimes she tortured herself with the thought that in some way she could have prevented her father's suicide. Was there a cry for help she had not heard? Most suicides give indications beforehand of what they are planning, so she had read. Somehow she had missed the signs. And had she done the right thing in lying to Ruth Ellen about his death, saying it was a heart attack? But Ruth Ellen had been through so much already and she was only trying to spare her the unpleasant details, which could only upset her more. But to her mother she had told the truth. She had made him suffer and she deserved it.

Well, all that was in the past now and there was nothing she could do about it. From here on in she had to concentrate on what she was going to do with her life.

"Look at that little yellow bird sitting on that ladder." The doctor pointed. "It must have flown all the way out here from shore to greet us with a song. There's an old Chinese saying, 'If I keep a green bough in my heart, the singing bird will come.' There's our singing bird."

"Perhaps it's a good omen," Marcia said. "I hope so."

Ruth Ellen put the snapshots in the envelope with the letter and before sealing it she read over again what she had written to Peter's mother. It was so hard to know what to say to her, especially as she had heard nothing from her since the baby was born three months ago.

But she was the only grandparent little Peter had left and she wanted him to know her.

"Don't give up on Nina," Lathrop Spaulding had told her the last time she saw him. "She'll come around eventually." He had been so kind and generous to her, given her a large check and set up a trust fund for the baby. She had looked forward to visits with him and his death had come as a terrible shock. Marcia wrote her that he'd had a heart attack at his apartment in New York and that when they found him there was nothing to be done, he was already gone.

She looked over at her son sleeping peacefully in his crib. In two weeks they would be moving to Houston and she would be glad to get away from Midland and all its painful memories. She must put it all behind her. Her new job was in an attorney's office in Houston where a girlfriend worked, one she'd gone to high school with in Fort Worth, so she would at least have someone to introduce her around. But it was so hard to pick up the pieces, to even imagine the rest of her life without Peter.

The baby stirred and started to cry. It was time for his bottle. She had wanted to breastfeed him and had even tried to in the beginning, but she didn't have enough milk and finally she had to give up and put him on a formula.

She picked him up and cradled him in her arms. How adorable he was, how sweet and trusting. She changed his diaper and then put his bottle in a pan on the stove to warm it. He started to howl with hunger.

"Just a minute, my angel, I'm bringing it."

She tested a drop of milk on her wrist. "Here we are. It's just right." She popped the nipple into his mouth and sat down in a rocking chair with him as he sucked hungrily. Tornado came over and lay down at her feet looking up at them. At first he had been jealous of the newcomer, but now he was as devoted to little Peter as he had been to his master and acted very protective toward him.

"You're such a good dog," she told Tornado, who thumped his tail happily.

She put the baby over her shoulder and burped him, then continued giving him the bottle, rocking back and forth gently in the chair.

❖

Nina took the letter out of the drawer in her desk and looked at the snapshots. Then she read the letter one more time:

> *Dear Senhora Carvalho,*
>
> *I am sending you some snapshots of the baby, which I thought you might like to see. He is such a darling and sleeps through the night now. Every day he looks more and more like his father. Perhaps I am prejudiced, but I think he is a beautiful baby. I know you would love him and I hope you will get to know each other in the future.*
>
> *In two weeks we are moving to Houston where I have a job as a secretary to an attorney in a large law firm. Enclosed is our new address. I have sold the house here in Midland and am busy getting everything packed up.*
>
> *Your little grandson sends you his love and so do I.*
>
> *Ruth Ellen*

Nina felt tears filling her eyes and she put down the letter and wiped them away. It was true, he did resemble Peter as a baby and all of a sudden she felt an aching longing to hold him in her arms.

If only Roberto were not so unreasonable about children. She had neglected her children for him and she had been punished. She had not been a good mother, but perhaps now she was being given another chance.

She put the snapshots of little Peter on the table beside her bed. She would go to Houston in about a month and visit them. She took out her notepaper and was starting to write a letter to Ruth Ellen when she heard Roberto.

"*Querida.*" He came over and kissed her on the back of her neck. "I see you are busy writing a letter."

She turned. "I heard from Ruth Ellen today and she sent me some snapshots of the baby. They're on my bedside table."

He glanced over and frowned

"I want to go to Houston and see them," Nina said.

"Do you think that is a good idea?"

"Why not? We could go together, stop in New York on the way, go to the theatre. Wouldn't you like that?"

"It is a possibility. Let me think it over."

"Please, Roberto. I want to see him so much. I didn't even realize how much until now." She brushed away a tear. "He is all I have left of Peter."

"If it would mean that much to you, my dearest, we shall go. It is my greatest desire to see you happy again."

"Oh, Roberto, thank you!" She threw her arms around him and kissed him. "I love you," she said.

She was starring on Broadway as the ingenue in the new play by John van Druten and her reviews had been excellent. She was a success, Valerie thought, and yet there was a hollow space inside her that no amount of applause could satisfy.

Peter. The baby I murdered, or so Catholics would call it, I suppose. But I am not a Catholic, so why do I feel guilty, why do I want to cry whenever I see a baby, thinking of Peter's baby and mine, or what would have been our baby, the child I will never know. That stifling hot summer day outside Baltimore, the shabby office and the heavy-set nurse holding me, the white sheet hiding the doctor's face, the scraping. . . .

Why do they want to make you feel so guilty?

I did what had to be done and it is over. And yet. . . .

It is too late for regrets. Peter is dead. Someday I will love again, I will have a child, but now I have my career. Everything is useful as an actress, so they say, pain can be used, the lonely childhood, the tragic love affair, all this will make me a better actress.

And so the curtain rises on another performance, I am ready, this is my life now, my real life, all the rest is memory.

THIRTY-TWO

*T*he truck driver tried to see through the thick fog as he drove along the highway between Midland and Odessa, but the visibility was almost zero. He couldn't see the white center line at all and he could barely make out the road. There was a line of cars behind him crawling slowly, their lights reflected in the side mirror of his cab. It was nights like this he'd like to be home in bed instead of out on the road, but with a wife and three kids to feed, he had no choice. This delivery of fuel oil was going to be late, he thought, but there wasn't nothing he could do about it.

Billie was laughing as she snuggled up to Earl in the car, her hand caressing his knee. "It's like floating in the clouds," she said. "As if we're the only two people in the world."

Earl scowled and peered through the windshield. "Cut it out, will ya? I gotta concentrate on my driving. It's hard enough as it is in this fog."

Billie's chatter was beginning to get on his nerves. He must've been plumb crazy to ever have mentioned marriage to her and she'd been bringing it up ever since Jo Beth died. No way, he thought. Billie didn't fit into his future plans.

"Hand me a cloth or something," he said. "These windshield wipers aren't doing much good. It's fogging up faster than they're working."

Yeah, he'd done all right, he thought, for a poor boy from the hill country whose daddy didn't have two nickels to rub together. He smiled. You could get anything if you knew how to pull the right strings. And he'd covered his tracks, old Earl had. He could just picture himself in the governor's mansion in Austin. Nothing was going to stop him now.

Billie opened her purse and took out a handkerchief and handed it to Earl.

"For Christ's sake, is that all you can find?" He tried to clean the window but it was a useless effort.

"I think I'll have to pull off the road until this fog lifts," he said. "I can't see a damned thing."

Just then Billie screamed as headlights appeared directly in front of them. "Earl, watch out! It's a truck!"

Those were her last words as the heavy truck crunched the black Cadillac like a matchbox.

The driver climbed down from the cab of his truck and looked in the window of the crushed car. What he saw made him want to puke. Both occupants were obviously dead. A man was pinned behind the steering wheel, his eyes open and staring sightlessly with blood running down his face. The red-haired woman with him had been thrown halfway through the windshield and her head was practically decapitated. He turned and threw up the chili and frankfurters he had eaten at the last truck stop and kept retching and retching even after his stomach was empty.

EPILOGUE

*A*fter Roberto's lingering death from lung cancer, Nina moved back to Washington and left Rio and that life far behind her. She lives now in a narrow red brick house covered with ivy on a quiet street in Georgetown.

It is a charming old house and Nina has put her special stamp on it. Entering the marble-tiled hallway, one looks past the stairs to the drawing room and French windows which open onto a flower-filled courtyard with a fountain. In the drawing room the late afternoon sun filters through the red and gold leaves of the trees outside onto the pale green silk hangings, which frame the windows and cover the walls of the room. Two giltwood Italian armchairs are upholstered in green velvet and between them is a needlepoint footstool on which a fluffy white cat is sleeping. A heavy Brazilian desk of dark ornately-carved jacarandá stands in one corner with a portrait of Nina above it, Nina in her younger years at the height of her beauty. The sofa is covered in ivory brocade, and a bronze bust of Marie Antoinette that Nina bought on one of her trips to Paris sits on a table with a framed antique fan and a vase of pink and white carnations.

Nina has finally surrendered to the battle of time and fine lines trace the years across her face, but the blue-green almond-shaped eyes glow with a determined light and the scent of "Bellodgia" hangs in the air as she enters the room.

They will be here any minute—Ruth Ellen, her lawyer husband Josh, and grandson Peter, who has gone to pick them up at Dulles Airport. Nina sits in one of the green velvet armchairs and reaches for a cigarette in the box she brought from Rio covered in iridescent butterfly wings. She keeps meaning to stop smoking, but then she reminds herself that several of her friends who have done so have also gained a lot of weight and she still prides herself on her slim figure. The cat yawns and stretches, then starts to lick itself. Nina leans back in the chair inhaling the tobacco, remembering the years with Lathrop and the years that followed with Roberto, and now she is alone, as most women are alone in the end. Sometimes at night she wakes up reaching out for Roberto only to realize that he is gone, gone from her forever. She has forgotten the moments of tormented jealousy he caused her and she thinks only of how much she loved him, how happy she was with him. A woman will forgive a man anything if he is a good lover, and Roberto was that.

The doorbell rings and she hears the footsteps of her maid in the hall going to open the door. Nina quickly stubs out her cigarette in the green jade ashtray and goes to greet them in the entry hall.

"Ruth Ellen, my dear." They embrace and then Nina turns to Ruth Ellen's husband, a tall, rugged-looking Texan with graying hair. "How are you, Josh? Did you have a good flight from Houston?"

"Not bad."

"I just love those club-mobiles they have at Dulles," Ruth Ellen said. "It's such fun to ride in them."

"Let Maggie show you your room and take your things upstairs," Nina said. "And then we'll have a drink here before we go to the Sulgrave Club for dinner."

"Sounds good to me," Josh said.

Nina turned to Peter. "Will you help me with the drinks?"

"I'd be glad to."

"Your mother's looking so well," Nina said, as she and Peter walked to the bar. Over the years Ruth Ellen had become like a daughter to her, closer than her own daughter Marcia.

"Yes, Mom doesn't seem to age at all," Peter said. "But then neither do you, Nina," he quickly added. When Peter was small she asked him to call her Nina instead of Grandmother, and he has continued to do so.

Nina smiled at the compliment. What a handsome young man he is, she thought looking at him, tall, slender, with deep blue eyes and dark brown hair. And good manners as well, most unusual these days. "You flatter me," she said. "But keep it up, I like it. I'm really going to miss you when you leave for Suriname."

"I'll visit you whenever I come back to the States."

"Your room will always be ready for you. And bring any friend you'd like."

They heard Ruth Ellen and Josh coming down the stairs and Peter carried the tray of drinks into the drawing room.

"It was so sweet of you to let Peter stay with you while he was taking his State Department training for his new post," Ruth Ellen said.

"I've loved having him. The house is going to seem very empty without him."

"I wasn't even sure where Suriname was when Peter told me," Ruth Ellen said laughing. "I thought it was one of those new African countries until I looked it up on a map and found it was in South America."

"It used to be called Dutch Guiana," Nina said.

"And I've been studying hard learning Dutch," Peter said, handing his mother and stepfather a drink. "Hope the natives can understand me when I get there!"

"How long will you be posted in Suriname?" Josh asked.

"Two years. Then if I do a good job there as vice consul, I hope to get sent to Amsterdam or The Hague."

"And we'll come visit you there, won't we, Josh?" Ruth Ellen said. "I've always wanted to see those fields of tulips blooming in the spring in Holland."

"You mean you aren't coming to Suriname, Mom? I'll give you and Dad a nice tour of the jungles and swamplands and the bauxite mines and rubber plantations."

"Suriname's right on the Equator, isn't it?" Josh asked. "It must get pretty hot there."

"No hotter than parts of Texas in the summer," Peter kidded.

"It's too bad you just missed Marcia," Nina said. "She was here last week."

"Oh, I'm sorry not to have seen her," said Ruth Ellen. "Is she still involved with that shelter for battered women in Santa Monica?"

"Very much so. In fact she came to Washington to try to raise more funds for it and to see about starting other shelters around the country. You should look her up the next time you're in Los Angeles. She has a horse ranch in Malibu."

"Josh has to go to Los Angeles on business next month, don't you, darling?" Ruth Ellen said. "And I was planning to go along."

"Remind me to give you Marcia's new telephone number before you leave," Nina said. "It seems that everyone out there has an unlisted number."

"Aunt Marcia's a lot of fun," Peter said.

"I know. I wish we all didn't live so far apart so we could get together more often," Ruth Ellen said.

"And now I want to propose a toast," said Nina, raising her glass. "To Peter, and the beginning of a very successful career in the foreign service."

They lifted their glasses. "To Peter."

Nina looked at him with adoration. How well he has turned out, she thought proudly, and how much he resembles his father. It is almost as if her son has come back to life and she has been given a second chance.

www.ingramcontent.com/pod-product-compliance
Lightning Source LLC
Chambersburg PA
CBHW031059020726
47495CB00007B/1956